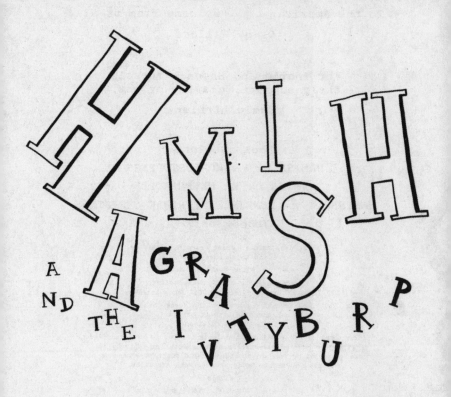

HAMISH
AND THE GRAVITY BURP

D1026189

To the American . . . welcome from us all!

Danny Wallace

For Ingrid and Shaun - for all
their support, gravity or not.

Jamie Littler

Look out for...

HAMISH AND THE WORLDSTOPPERS

HAMISH AND THE NEVERPEOPLE

HAMISH AND THE TERRIBLE TERRIBLE CHRISTMAS

(eBook only)

First published in Great Britain in 2017 by
Simon & Schuster UK Ltd

A CBS COMPANY

Text copyright © 2017 Danny Wallace
Illustrations copyright © 2017 Jamie Littler

This book is copyright under the Berne Convention.
No reproduction without permission.
All rights reserved.

The right of Danny Wallace and Jamie Littler to be identified
as the author and illustrator of this work respectively has
been asserted by them in accordance with sections 77 and 78 of
the Copyright, Design and Patents Act, 1988.

1 3 5 7 9 10 8 6 4 2

Simon & Schuster UK Ltd
1st Floor, 222 Gray's Inn Road
London, WC1X 8HB

www.simonandschuster.co.uk

Simon & Schuster Australia, Sydney

Simon & Schuster India, New Delhi

A CIP catalogue record for this book is available from the
British Library.

PB ISBN 978-1-4711-4712-8
eBook ISBN 978-1-4711-4713-5

This book is a work of fiction. Names, characters, places and
incidents are either the product of the author's imagination
or are used fictitiously. Any resemblance to actual people
living or dead, events or locales is entirely coincidental.

Printed and bound by CPI Group (UK) Ltd, Croydon, CR0 4YY

Simon & Schuster UK Ltd are committed to sourcing paper that
is made from wood grown in sustainable forests and supports
the Forest Stewardship Council, the leading international
forest certification organisation. Our books displaying the
FSC logo are printed on FSC certified paper.

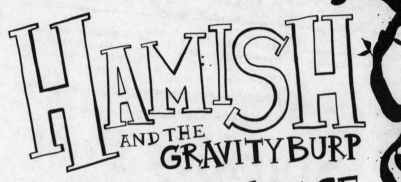

HAMISH
AND THE
GRAVITY BURP

BY DANNY WALLACE
ILLUSTRATED BY JAMIE LITTLER

SIMON & SCHUSTER
LONDON   NEW YORK   SYDNEY   TORONTO   NEW DELHI   STARKLEY

LORD OF THE FRIES

Now delivers to Port Fenland Nuclear Power Station

"Try the fission chips!"

12. Butcher gets new adder. The stakes are high!

P23. Free Brain Transplants? But what if you change your mind?

P83. Which of our puns made the year's Top Ten? Sadly, no pun in ten did. :(

BRITAIN'S FOURTH MOST BORING TOWN – AND PROUD OF IT!

Starkley Post

Price: 92p

Wednesday 2017 issue XX vol 12

ANOTHER VICTORY FOR THE PDF!

Starkley kids vanquish Scarmarsh!

'Hurrah for the PDF!' was the general feeling in Starkley today as local heroes the Pause Defence Force fought off another threat to life on Earth!

Evil villain Axel Scarmarsh may have escaped for now – but he won't be back in a hurry thanks to the efforts of Hamish Ellerby and friends.

'I really think that's the very last problem we'll ever have!' said local resident Boppo Rix, as quite without warning he began to float into the air. 'Yes, I can't see anything else happening for a while!'

If anyone knows the current whereabouts of Mr. Rix, please call the local police, as we lost sight of him as he drifted quickly over Frinkley.

"mainly because it was recently over... monsters wh...

QUIZFACE

It's quiz night at the Queen's Leg on Tuesdays. Can you answer this week's big questions?

1. I am a man from history. You know me as Napoleon Boneparte. But who am I?

2. A girl with seven arms walks into a room with two doors. But which one and how?

3. A five letter anagram, but you have to guess the letters. (6)

4. Pick a card, any card. Memorise it. Is it the one I'm thinking of? Yes. Now work out how.

Answers: 1. Napoleon Bonaparte 2. Any door, it is totally up to her. 3. As written. 4. Four of hearts

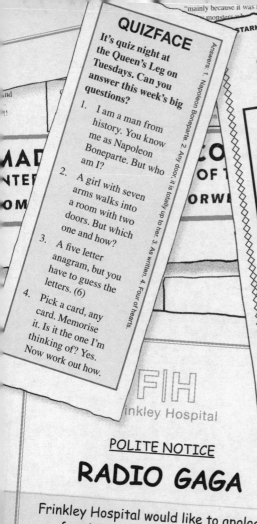

MAD
NTER
OM

CO
OF T
ORWE

FIH
inkley Hospital

POLITE NOTICE

RADIO GAGA

Frinkley Hospital would like to apologise for the loss of a nice clear radio signal outside the maternity ward – especially to anyone trying to listen to the Janice Mad show on Starkley FM.

Mind you, we would also like to apologise to anyone who heard the Janice Mad show who would have preferred to have lost their signal.

One thing's for sure – don't blame the babies!

STARKLEY TOWN COUNCIL TOURIST GUIDE

Come and see...

Starkley Town Clock!

Are you thinking about seeing Starkley Town Clock? Probably not, so here are reasons you should:

1. It's a great clock if you like clocks
2. Especially if you like completely normal clocks
3. By which we mean completely normal clocks that have nothing out of the ordinary about them at all!

"So if you like normal clocks, and aren't expecting anything unusual about this clock, come and see this clock, which is a normal clock and has nothing at all unusual about it!"™

0

Oh!

Oh, it's **YOU!**

I recognise you.

Do you know how?

From your grubby little fingerprints when you first picked up this book.

I knew then and there it was you!

There was the smell too, of course. I don't have to tell you that you have a very *distinct* smell. A very *unusual* aroma. A wonderfully *unique* bouquet.

But, in the interest of politeness, I think it might be best to ignore your incredible stink for now.

Anyway, I bet you're wondering how a simple book could recognise your fingerprints and pick up on your stink, so let me tell you.

Sometimes you might think the thing you're looking at is just a thing that you're looking at.

You might think that thing is normal. That it's completely and utterly ordinary.

But wait – look a little closer, and you might find that it's . . .

Special.

Lots of things are like that. Books. Places. People. Your mum's awful cooking.

Each one has something really special about it. OK, maybe not your mum's cooking.

So, yes, this book may look like it's just a normal, completely and utterly ordinary book.

But it's not.

It's a book written just for you.

That's right. Before you picked it up and flicked through it, none of the words and pictures were here. In fact, the whole book was blank, just waiting for you . . .

Because this book is your ticket into a secret organisation.

And this book knows all about YOU.

It knows that the other day you had cake. It knows your birthday is less than a year away. It knows that secretly you love your mum's cooking.

And this book also knows something terrifying: that the people of Earth face their gravest, grimmest threat yet.

A threat so grave and so grim that if I just came out and told you what it was, your hair would turn white, your teeth would fall out, your legs would turn into apples and you'd marry a cat.

So, in the interests of you not marrying a cat, let me start by telling you what's happening in the small, normal, completely and utterly ordinary town of Starkley. A town you may already be familiar with. One which has had to deal with some very unusual occurrences over the past few months. And the same town in which Hamish Ellerby, a normal, completely and utterly ordinary ten-year-old boy, has just returned home . . .

. . . to find that something absolutely *extraordinary was happening.*

Up, Up
and Wahey!

Hamish Ellerby burst through the door of his home and was shocked to find his mum and brother lying flat on their backs.

Both of them. Flat on their backs.

Flat on their backs . . . *on the ceiling!*

'Help! We're stuck up here!' Jimmy shouted, looking panicked and confused, because being stuck on the ceiling doesn't happen to big brothers that often. 'Why are we stuck on the ceiling?'

It wasn't just them up there either. There was a bowl of fruit too. Six batteries. And a wind-up meerkat.

A disgusting, bleurghy sound bowled through the small town of Starkley, rattling teacups and dentures in glasses.

∪∪∪∪∪∪∪∪URRRRRRRRRRRRRRP!

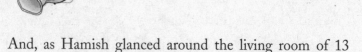

And, as Hamish glanced around the living room of 13
Lovelock Close, more objects
were rising up, up, up into
the air.

Vases! Cushions!
Magazines!

The TV remote! A pencil!
Mum's packet of chocolate
Mustn'tgrumbles!

All of them gently drifting
upwards, spookily lifting off from chairs and coffee
tables – that were now starting to slowly rise up
themselves.

Pictures and frames left their hooks
and scraped their way up the walls.

Every carpet fibre stood to attention and shook.

The TV was just floating in mid-air, straining against the
plug in the wall, like a dog pulling at its leash.

'What's going ON?' yelled Mum. 'I can't hang
around on the ceiling all day – I've
got things to DO!'

This was NOT NORMAL.

Hamish and his dad had been sitting on the grass by the town square when it had started.

Hamish noticed it first: a small chocolate bar had started twitching on the ground beside him. Then a can began to float near a bin. He'd watched a football shoot off into the atmosphere like a firework, then the leaves from trees start to break away and fly straight upwards too. It was amazing. It was beautiful somehow. He could have stayed there all day and watched this weirdness.

It was when he could feel himself getting lighter too that his dad had pulled him towards the safety of home.

'Hamish!' shouted his mum, now splayed out like an upside-down starfish. 'You're rising too!'

WHAT?

Hamish looked at his feet. They weren't on the floor any more. He tried to run, but his feet had nothing to run on and, as his legs spun wildly around like he was swimming in the air, he grabbed onto his dad. The two of them began to float quickly up to the ceiling!

'Oi! Get off!' shouted Jimmy, as Hamish drifted up and lay flat across him. 'I need my space!'

Jimmy was fifteen and always going on about how he needed his space.

'I can't help it!' said Hamish, face to face with him. 'Gravity's gone funny! It's happening all over town!'

Now Hamish's messy mop of hair was getting in Jimmy's nostrils.

'Get your hair out of my face!' yelled Jimmy.

'Get your face out of my hair!' yelled Hamish.

'**Aaaachoooo!**' sneezed Jimmy, and a long trail of bright yellow snot flew from his nose and missed Hamish by millimetres.

'That was close,' said Hamish, relieved. 'You nearly used me as a hankie!'

But gravity had plans for that long trail of snot.

As it spun towards the floor, it slooooooowed, stopped, then began to rise, doubling back towards them.

'The snot's coming back!' yelled Jimmy, trying to push Hamish in its way. 'The snot wants revenge!'

It was like a creepy, thin snake, climbing high into the air, getting closer, closer, closer, twirling and turning and sloppy and wet . . .

Hamish and Jimmy scrabbled against one another, desperate to get out of the way of the levitating snot snake.

And then, like there had been a thunderclap no one could hear, the spell was broken.

'Watch out!' yelled Hamish's dad, as all four members of the Ellerby family hung for a second, then came crashing back down to the ground.

Hamish landed in an armchair.

Jimmy landed heavily on top of him.

Mum and Dad bounced off the sofa and onto the floor.

Vases crashed after them. The TV fell and fizzed and cracked. The room rained cushions and magazines and pencils and wind-up meerkats.

And, a second or so later, that long, wet trail of snot slopped itself across Jimmy's hair and face.

'I **SLIMED** myself!' he wailed, horrified.

For a moment more, everything was quiet.

Then the bangs started. Small ones at first.

Bang! Bang! Bang!

'What's that?' said Hamish, worried, creeping closer to his mum for protection. Her hair was pointing in the air, like a mad punk. She'd been using hairspray just before the gravity had changed and now it had set that way.

'Look outside,' said his dad, and Hamish pressed his face up against the window.

BANG! BANG! BANG!

Apples that had shot up into the air were now on their way back down, and bouncing off the roofs of Lovelock Close.

BANG! BANG!
BANG BANG BANG!

Anything that hadn't been nailed down had gone up, up, up and was now coming down, down, down. Pine cones. Coke cans. Shoes. Footballs. Bins. Garden chairs. Last night's macaroni pizza.

Hamish watched, wide-eyed, as across the street bicycles crashed to Earth.

Car alarms went off.

A cat landed in a pond.

Mr Ramsface was clinging to the guttering next door and shouting words he really should not be shouting.

'Right!' said Hamish's dad, reaching for the phone. 'This calls for a town meeting.'

And, as phones began to ring all over the place, the people of Starkley crept out of their homes to stare up at the skies, curious and frightened.

Not a single one of them could have known that things were about to get much, much worse.

Things Get Worse

Starkley was in an absolute ding-dong.

Nothing was in its proper place any more. Nothing was where it should have been.

It looked like your room.

'What on earth just happened?' yelled Madame Cous Cous, waving her stick around as she bundled into Winterbourne School hall. 'My whole sweet shop is upside down! There are Cantonese Caramel Carbuncles all over the ceiling! Next-door's dog flew through my window and 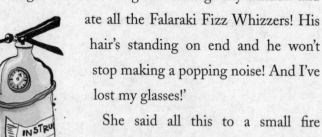 ate all the Falaraki Fizz Whizzers! His hair's standing on end and he won't stop making a popping noise! And I've lost my glasses!'

She said all this to a small fire extinguisher she must have thought was a very short, red-faced man.

'Your glasses have floated up into your hair!' said Hamish's teacher, Mr Longblather, whose usually droopy moustache was now pointing straight at his eyebrows. 'And never mind that popping dog. Poor little Manjit Singhdaliwal floated off and ended up in a tree in Frinkley! We had to send two fire engines to get him down!'

The people of Starkley were in a panic. Everyone felt extremely unsettled, as you might expect when the very laws of nature have been unexpectedly trifled with.

'And what was that disgusting noise?' demanded Winterbourne School's head teacher, Frau Fussbundler. 'That huge massive **UUUURRRRRRP** sound? I thought Grenville Bile had food poisoning again.'

Hamish stayed at the side of the room with his dad. Dad hadn't said much since they arrived at the town meeting; he just stood there with a dark expression on his face, like he was thinking something through.

Over in the corner, Mr Slackjaw had a big white bandage wrapped round his head where he'd bopped it on the ceiling of his garage, Slackjaw's Motors. It would have been okay, he said, if, when the world had gone back to normal, all his spanners hadn't then rained down on his bonce.

Just like everyone else, Mr Slackjaw had lots of questions.

Why had his spanners all flown up into the air? Why had they all fallen straight down again? Did his spanners hate him? Unlike everyone else, all his questions were about spanners.

More and more people arrived with more and more questions. Did you see? What happened to you? Could it happen again? The hubbub and chatter got noisier and noisier.

All of this was particularly confusing because, as you might know, Starkley used to be such a very boring town indeed. It had been a town in which nothing ever happened and no one had anything to talk about. If it had been a colour, it would have been Yawn Brown. If it had been a biscuit, it would have been a Belgian Bore-bon.

But, just recently, things had changed. Now Starkley was a town in which lots of things went on. It had been at the centre of a *WorldStoppers invasion*, overrun by shadowy, creepy monsters called the *Terribles*. And also where Hamish and his friends had come up with a plan to stop an evil mastermind from taking over TWO universes at once. All in all, it had been an eventful few months. Far from being boring, Starkley was now a town where Hamish and his best friend Alice had to always be ready to think quickly in case another new disaster was about to befall it.

Actually – where was Alice? If there was a time for collective quick thinking, it was now, but Hamish couldn't see—

'ALWAYS BE PREPARED!' came a voice, quite suddenly, and Hamish jumped as Alice slapped him on the back of his head.

'What are you doing?' said Hamish, shocked.

'Getting ready!' said Alice, delighted, kneeling down to tie the laces of her cherry-red army boots. 'It's exciting! Something's happening, Hamish! Something involving the laws of space and time and gravity and whatnot. We need to get everyone in the **PDF** together to figure out what's going on. The greatest minds in Starkley! And Venk!'

She leapt up again and struck a karate pose. Then she relaxed and took out a nut and pickle baguette from her combat shorts and started to munch.

Alice was the founding member of the **Pause Defence Force** – also known as the **PDF** – the gang Hamish and his closest friends belonged to. She hated being bored. It was so boring. To her, any strange occurrence meant one thing: adventure. And, if adventure was coming, that meant two more things:

1. You had to be prepared.
2. You had to prepare a sandwich.

Hamish, on the other hand, really felt like a rest. It had been ages since he'd just sat down and read a comic, or eaten a Chomp and watched telly. Sometimes he missed just being a kid. And it had only been about forty minutes since his last adventure!

'What's going on, Hamish?' said his friend Buster, walking in. 'I was in Mum's ice-cream van when it happened.

Suddenly all the Flakes shot out of the cones like bullets and splatted on the ceiling!'

'Something is definitely up,' said Elliot, walking in and adjusting his spectacles. 'No pun intended.'

'None taken,' said Clover, the **PDF**'s master of disguise, following behind. Clover had obviously sensed things weren't right and immediately raided her disguise box. She was now dressed as half-spy (in case she might need to be a spy) and half-pirate (in case she might need to be a pirate).

Hamish also had questions that needed answers, and he knew the man to ask.

'Hey, Dad . . .' he said, turning round, but his dad wasn't there any more. He was standing at the front of the hall with his hands behind his back and a very grim expression on his face.

'Ladies and gentlemen, I have some news for you,' he said, loudly, and everyone hushed up and turned to stare. 'What we just experienced here in Starkley . . . was a **GravityBurp**.'

'A . . . a what?' someone said.

Elliot whipped his pad out and started to make notes.

'A GravityBurp. A momentary blip in gravity. A few seconds where everything is different and all the rules have changed.'

Alice nudged Hamish and raised her eyebrows.

See? Adventure! she seemed to be saying.

But Hamish's dad had already told him about GravityBurps. His dad, you see, was a member of something called **Belasko**: a super-special agency that operates secretly here on Earth, doing their best to keep our planet safe and secure from any threats whatsoever. Bad guys. Aliens. Monsters. Geography teachers. Babies that stink. Anyone.

Hamish loved his dad so much. Not long ago, his dad had disappeared from the family home. He'd popped out to buy ice cream and crisps and didn't come back. No one knew where he'd gone, or why. Now Hamish knew that his dad

had to leave because he was trying to protect his family. But when his dad had left, Hamish had stared out of his living-room window for weeks, waiting for him to come home. Hamish had been overwhelmingly sad. He'd been anxious. He'd also been angry. Very angry. But he'd always tried never to let any of this show. And now he was just pleased to have his dad back.

'So, here's the problem,' continued Hamish's dad. 'If we've experienced one GravityBurp, you can bet we're going to experience another. Perhaps more than one. And – what's more – they're going to get worse.'

Alice squeezed Hamish's hand.

'We need to tie everything down!' yelled Madame Cous Cous, still addressing that fire extinguisher. 'We need nails! And string! And parachutes!' The fire extinguisher didn't reply. Madame Cous Cous had had enough of its rudeness so whacked it with her stick.

'We're going to have to work together,' said Hamish's dad. 'We're going to have to move fast, not panic and think on our feet. We're going to have to—'

But he stopped talking as the doors of Winterbourne School opened with a **BANG**.

Everyone jumped. In fact, the whole room seemed to shake.

In the doorway stood a tall, sniffy, narrow-shouldered woman with a large nose and a fearsome expression. But the oddest thing about her was that she was wearing a neck cone. The sort you see on dogs when they come out of the vet's.

The woman stared at the people of Starkley. The people of Starkley stared at her.

She had a blush of angry pink hair combed into a proud and enormous beehive. She wore a flowery green dress and a string of old pearls that looked like they'd rather be

anywhere else. Without breaking eye contact, she pulled out a clipboard from her alligator handbag, adjusted her neck cone and began to speak.

'Good, you're all here,' she said, then began to walk slowly towards the stage.

CLUMP CLUMP CLUMP went her heavy feet. The floorboards squeaked under her weight. She reminded Hamish of Grenville Bile's favourite Mexican wrestler, El Gamba.

'I didn't get a reply to my letter,' she said, and everyone turned to look at Grenville's blushing mum, who had gained a reputation over the years for only delivering maybe 3 per cent of Starkley's letters. 'But I see you are all here anyway. So let's begin.'

Literally nobody knew who this woman was or why she was here. But everyone decided the safest thing to do would be to just play along. She seemed important and like she was here for a reason. She certainly seemed to think she was in charge. Best just pretend and let her get on with things.

'My name, as you know, is Goonhilda Swag,' she said, staring into people's eyes from the stage as she stamped slowly around. Every time she stopped, it took a moment for her beehive hairdo to stop swaying.

'I am here because Her Majesty the Queen recently decided to rename Starkley and call it "Royal Starkley".'

Everyone breathed a sigh of relief. That was true. And that's why Goonhilda thought everyone was gathered here today. The Queen had been so impressed the last time Starkley saved the world that she'd said that from now on it would have a far more regal name. Today must be the day this strange woman was going to make the name change official. This was deeply exciting.

'HOWEVER!' said Goonhilda, her pink beehive wobbling and flobbling. 'The Queen is not the only person in charge of these things. I am. And I have to tell you, from what I have seen and heard of your "town", I am not happy.'

Everyone gasped. What on earth could she say was wrong with Starkley?

'The recent events I've been told have happened in Starkley were bad enough, but on my way in just now,' said Goonhilda, cracking a knuckle, 'I counted three old men stuck in trees. That is well above the national average. I also counted six bins upside down. I saw a car spinning on its roof. There is litter everywhere.'

Well, yes, but . . . that wasn't Starkley's fault! That was the GravityBurp! Talking of which, what if there was another one in a moment? They needed to prepare. They should warn Goonhilda!

Someone put their hand up to try and tell her there was something a bit more important going on, but Goonhilda was having none of it.

'SHOOSH YOUR LIPS!' she barked, folding her arms behind her back. 'Now I've read about this town, and I have to say there have been some very odd things happening here indeed. Some. Very. Odd. Things.'

The CLUMPs of her feet seemed louder and more foreboding now. She was talking slowly. Almost snarling. Relishing every word. Hamish could tell that this was a woman who enjoyed being the centre of attention. She liked people being scared of her. She was thrilled by the power she had over Starkley.

'I come from the government's Public Office of Pride,' she said, fiddling with her neck cone, and looking rather pleased with herself. 'Or POP.'

Mr Slackjaw raised his hand.

Goonhilda sighed. 'Fine. One question. What is it, Bandage Bonce?' she barked.

'Shouldn't it be . . .' – he swallowed nervously, before quietly saying – 'POOP?'

Goonhilda grimaced.

'Public Office of Pride. POP!'

That told him.

'But, um, there are two "o" words,' said Mr Slackjaw, and people started to shuffle slowly away from him. 'So it's POOP.'

'It's not POOP because we don't count the second "o", so it's POP!' said Goonhilda, moving towards him, menacingly.

'I think it's probably POOP,' he shrugged.

'It's not POOP! It's POP!'

'I just think you're from POOP.'

'You're POOP! I'm POP! And I am afraid it's my terrible duty to inform you that in the opinion of POOP . . .'

She kicked herself.

'I mean, in the opinion of POP, not only do I feel that Starkley should not be renamed Royal Starkley . . .'

Everyone gasped again.

'. . . but, as far as POOP – POP! – is concerned, there is a very strong case for having Starkley taken off the map altogether!'

She put her hands on her hips, triumphant, and stared straight at Mr Slackjaw.

'What?' shouted Madame Cous Cous. 'You can't take Starkley off the map!'

Sadly though, and despite Mr Longblather trying to help her, she still hadn't found her glasses and said all this to a small potted plant on a shelf.

'I am Goonhilda Swag and I can and I will, you mad little woman!' shrieked Goonhilda.

'Hamish,' whispered Alice, as Goonhilda kept on ranting. 'What time is it?'

Why did she want to know what the time was? Where did she have to be?

'We can't have towns like Starkley making the rest of the country look bad!' yelled Goonhilda over the growing noise and angry murmurings in the school hall. 'Far better to take you off the map where no one will ever find you than advertise the fact that you people exist.'

She spat out the words 'you people' with such scorn that they could have burnt a hole wherever they landed. But even though taking Starkley off the map would be a terrible thing to happen – how would anyone ever find them? Who wants to live in a place that doesn't exist? – Hamish was distracted by Alice's odd question.

'Why do you want to know what time it is?' he asked, as Alice looked quizzically around the room. What had she noticed?

'In fact, I have to tell you,' Goonhilda went on, holding up her clipboard, 'I'm close to signing the document to make that happen right now. Oh, I'll have to tell the Queen, of course, but as soon as I mention the old men stuck up trees I'm sure she'll see the light. In fact, I'm so close that if just one more strange thing happens . . .'

Until Alice's interruption, Hamish had been listening quite intently. It all seemed so unfair. So unjust! But now he realised that something was changing as Goonhilda spoke.

'. . . even if it's just one more out-of-the-ordinary little thing that makes Starkley stand out . . .'

Now nobody was listening to the massive bully in the awful dress. Everyone was looking around the room, making curious faces at one another, glancing at the windows, whispering . . .

'. . . then I am afraid that your town will be taken out of the guidebooks and off the maps, and—'

'WHO TURNED OUT THE LIGHTS?'

screamed Madame Cous Cous, because suddenly it was dark. Actually, it was really dark.

And, what's more, it was getting darker.

'Hamish, LOOK!' shouted Alice who was now standing by the window and pointing towards the sky. Hamish ran over to her and the look on her face told Hamish that whatever Alice had seen had scared the daylights out of her.

In fact, whatever Alice had seen had scared the daylight out of Starkley.

3

The Living
Daylights

Fifteen seconds later, Hamish and Alice had run outside and were standing bravely in the darkening playground to get a closer look at whatever was happening.

Most of the grown-ups had stayed indoors, cowering by the windows, turning their backs on an increasingly frustrated Goonhilda Swag.

They'd all been so preoccupied with wondering if there'd be another GravityBurp that they just weren't prepared for this.

Day seemed to be turning to night.

But not everywhere – just right above Starkley.

In fact, if you were looking down at the world from above, it would have appeared just the way it normally did, except for a big dark spot where Starkley was.

To the left and to the right of the town, it was as bright as

you like. But immediately above the tiny figures of Hamish and Alice was a huge and ominous black cloud.

A huge, black, smoky cloud.

A huge, black, smoky, moving cloud.

'Do you hear that?' asked Alice, staring straight up, instinctively moving closer to her friend.

'What's that noise?' asked Buster, running out of the school hall towards them, the other members of the **PDF** following closely behind.

CCCCCCCHHHHHHHHH came the distant noise. Like the sound a radio makes when it isn't tuned properly.

Getting louder.

And louder.

From right above their heads.

CCCCCCCHHHHHHHHHHHH.

'It sounds . . . like a machine!' said Elliot. 'Or . . . insects?'

Now the double doors behind them were flung open, and the residents of Starkley poured out of the school hall in a panic.

'Who said INSECTS?' yelled Goonhilda Swag, thundering out and batting everyone else out of the way with her knobbly elbows. 'I HATE insects! Spiders! Dung beetles! The Mariachi Mayfly! Bungle Trumps! Booger Ticks! ALL OF THEM!'

'Run, children!' yelled Frau Fussbundler. 'It must be some kind of storm! Get home!'

'It doesn't look like a normal cloud,' said Elliot, standing completely still, totally fascinated. 'It's neither **cumulonimbus** nor **stratocumulus**!'

He smiled and tapped the others on the arm to point out just how weird that was, but nobody had the faintest idea what he was talking about.

The **CCCCCCCHHHHHHHHHH** was even louder now, like it was almost inside all of their ears.

'I think we need to get home,' said Hamish's mum, suddenly appearing.

But they'd never make it home in time.

Whatever this cloud was, it was indeed getting closer, and closer, and closer . . .

Do clouds fall to Earth?

Was this even a cloud?

Now it was so wide, and getting blacker, and looking angrier . . .

The wind rose and **CCCCCCCHHHHHHHHHHHH** came the noise, growing, roaring, until Hamish could see that actually this was not a cloud at all.

Whatever was headed to Earth was made up of billions and billions of tiny little dots.

'It is insects!' yelled Elliot.

'**AAAAARGH!**' cried Goonhilda.

But Hamish could tell Elliot was wrong. These weren't insects.

Then the first of the strange little things began landing around him. Little black dots clattered onto the ground, and skittered about, as more and more joined them. Clanging on roofs, battering benches and bollards and bushes and barnets . . .

Alice stooped to pick one up. It looked like a little black teardrop.

'SEEDS?' she said, holding it out so the others could see. 'Why are SEEDS falling from the sky?'

But they weren't just falling now. They were cascading down. Tumbling. So many seeds grouped together that they'd blocked out the very light that shone on Starkley.

The **CCCCCCHHHHH** turned to a **SSSSSSHHHHHH** like the fiercest rainstorm you've ever been in.

'Ow!' yelled Grenville Bile, running while trying to shield himself from the seeds and slamming straight into a lamp post.

'I'm covered!' yelled Buster. 'They're all in my hair!'

39

The seeds were falling with such ferocity that they were beginning to sting. They tore through the leaves left on the trees. They ricocheted off walls. If they didn't hit you on the way down, they got you when they bounced back up again.

'UNDER HERE!' yelled Clover over the noise, removing a seed from her nostril and opening up a small pink umbrella for the PDF to all cram themselves under.

Some people ran back inside the school. Others ran for the bus shelter. People dived through car windows as the seeds clattered and drummed against the roofs. Others hid in doorways and pulled their hoods up. Across Starkley, front doors slammed shut. All the while a trillion tiny seeds bounced and danced and pattered around on the concrete streets and hard tiles of the houses.

'This is HORRIBLE!' yelled Clover as they cowered under the umbrella.

And then, as quickly as it had begun . . .

SILENCE.

Sunshine.

Calm.

Clover carefully lowered the little pink umbrella and the kids peeked round it.

Everywhere was covered in a five-centimetre layer of little black seeds.

It was like snowfall. A really rubbish, crunchy black snowfall.

'Wh – what do you think they are?' said Hamish, kicking his feet, hearing seeds crunch and crackle underfoot.

He'd read once, in *THAT'S INTERESTING!* magazine, about strange things like this happening. It was to do with whirlwinds, they said, or maybe tornadoes. The article had said that sometimes, in a place called Honduras, it actually rains small, silvery, slithery fish. He'd also read that in Serbia, at least once a year, it rains frogs! And, apparently, if a tornado goes over a lake, it can suck up whatever's inside and carry it through the air for miles and miles until it loses power and just drops whatever it was carrying. But Hamish had never heard of it raining seeds anywhere. And it had certainly never happened in Starkley before.

Slowly, around town, doors opened again. People peered out of cars. Windows were pulled up and faces popped out. The grown-ups that had stayed in the school hall began to creep out again, to find that seeds now carpeted the town. They filled every gutter. Every brim of every hat. There were seeds in every nook and cranny of every nook and cranny.

'H, I think I know what this might be,' said Hamish's dad, holding one in the palm of his hand, and studying it very seriously.

And then, from right behind them . . .

'MMFF-MFFMMF! MMMFFF MFFMFMM!'

It was Goonhilda. She may have run off, but she hadn't made it back to the school in time. Her neck cone had filled right up with seeds so that they completely covered her mouth.

All you could see were two large and panicked eyes. Her plump little arms couldn't reach up to get rid of the seeds. She spun around, pirouetting, arms flailing wildly, trying to dislodge them and shout-mumbling all the while.

'MMFFF-MMMFFF!'

Goonhilda had seeds in her hair and seeds in her ears and, by the way, she had a not inconsiderable number of seeds in her pants too.

Finally, she bent straight forward and all the seeds poured out of the cone.

'MMMFF,' she said, then spat a huge great gobful of seeds all over poor Buster.

'That is IT!' she said, furious. 'That was the LAST STRAW!'

It was as if she had taken this seed storm very personally. Like it had been planned somehow to anger her and only her. This very self-centred woman whipped out her clipboard, shook all the seeds out of it and found a pen.

'I am writing an OFFICIAL REPORT!' she raged, pointing it at anyone she saw. 'You will all rue the day you messed with Goonhilda Swag!'

The people of Starkley looked rather upset at the idea of an official report on them, but if he was bothered Hamish's dad didn't show it.

Hamish knew the dark look on his dad's face meant that, right now, they had far bigger problems to deal with.

4

No One Seed
That Coming!

Hamish Ellerby, as you know, is a boy of action. When action is to be taken, Hamish will take it. No ifs, no buts, no maybes!

But sometimes he likes to make neat lists first.

He decided there were three very pressing things to deal with:

1. Clean up Starkley.

2. Prepare in case of another GravityBurp.

3. Work out why all this is happening!

Goonhilda Swag had left town in quite a hurry, shouting and bellowing and picking seeds out of her ears and flicking them at cats. So Hamish would worry about Goonhilda and the Public Office of Pride (which he agreed with Mr Longblather should be called POOP) later.

What was far more worrying were these seeds. What were they? Why had so many of them been dropped right on Starkley? And what would happen when they grew?

I mean, let's look on the bright side. They might be melon seeds. Everybody loves melons. But, even so, you don't want a whole town covered in billions of melons, do you? You don't want to become the 'melon' town. You don't want everyone calling you 'Old Melon Face the melon lover who loves melons and lives in MelonTown', do you? 'You know, Old Melon Face from MelonTown – the town that's all just melons! Ooh, they love melons there, they really do!'

How would you get anything done? You'd be eating melon for breakfast, lunch and tea. You'd have to drink melon juice all day long. You'd have to have a spare room, just full of melons, and sleep in a big melon bed, in among all the massive melon pips. Sooner or later, you'd go mad, because all you'd ever talk about would be melons, and all your friends would be melons.

But I've got sidetracked, because all of that is supposing these seeds were lovely, tasty melons. What if they were something else entirely?

What if these seeds were for ENORMOUS HUGE GREAT STINK TREES? Trees so big and so huge that suddenly you found yourself living in a massive, dark, stinky forest? And they grew underneath your house until one day you woke up and you were living at the very top of one of those enormous huge great trees with a clothes peg on your nose to block out the smell? Okay, you'd get a zip wire to school, and that would be fun, but how on earth would you get back up every night?

Or what if they turned into . . . sharp, spiky cactuses? And the whole town became a terrible health-and-safety risk? And you couldn't even leave your house without getting prodded and poked and grazed and scratched by awful spiky needles? Needles over there, needles in your hair. Needles in your shoes, needles in your poos. You'd have to wear a bubble-wrap suit, or roll around in a hamster ball, just so you didn't end up covered in plasters.

None of this sounds ideal, does it?

No. The seeds had to go. Whatever they were.

'What we need is some kind of **motorised centrifugal fan** capable of creating a form of instant partial vacuum to suck the seeds into a sort of **basic attached containment unit**,' said Elliot, scratching his head, then starting to work on possible designs on his pad.

'Do you mean . . . like a vacuum cleaner?' said a confused Clover, trying to get her head round it.

Elliot thought about it and stopped sketching.

'Yes,' he said.

'OKAY!' shouted Madame Cous Cous, slipping and skidding on the seeds. Things had become much more dangerous now the whole place was covered in the things. Then Madame Cous Cous realised she could actually use them to move around much quicker by paddling her big stick like an oar, and just punting herself around, pushing and sliding on the seeds as they rolled. **'OPERATION DE-SEEDING!'** she yelled, gliding past Hamish, looking like one of those gondoliers you see on boats in Venice. 'Positions, please!'

Anyone who owned a vacuum cleaner was now feeding extension lead after extension lead out of their window, pulling them across their lawn and plugging them in.

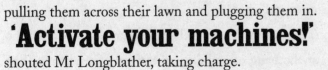

'Activate your machines!' shouted Mr Longblather, taking charge.

Hamish and his pals watched as dozens of vacuums of different shapes and sizes roared into life.

The high-pitched thrum of hoovering filled the air.

It sounded just like sports cars at the start of a big race.

'GO!' yelled Mr Longblather, and the seeds began to **RATTLE** and **CLATTER** up the vacuum-cleaner pipes and bounce around inside.

'Don't miss any of them!' yelled Madame Cous Cous, who had got the hang of walking on the sea of seeds now. She had her hands behind her back and looked like she was ice-skating along the pavement.

But, of course, it was impossible not to miss some of the seeds. Have you ever tried to clean up a bazillion tiny seeds?

Buster stumbled around as the seeds rolled and skipped and were generally impossible to control. Clover accidentally knocked some down into the sewers through a drain cover. Venk slipped and kicked some into Frau Fussbundler's trouser turn-ups. Other seeds were nestled up high, in chimneys or hanging baskets.

'What happens if we miss some?' said Alice, using a trowel to scoop a great pile of seeds up and place them in a Tupperware box.

'Then I suppose we'll soon know about it,' said Hamish, looking concerned.

It seemed an impossible task, but everyone agreed the important thing was to just try their best. Soon the paths were clear, the grass had been hoovered and everybody had checked everybody else's hair, the way monkeys look for nits.

Mr Slackjaw had filled up a whole lorry with the seeds and decided the best thing to do would be to pop them all in the sea. They were biodegradable, after all, and this way at least the fish might get a tasty treat.

'**STAGE TWO!**' yelled Madame Cous Cous, who really was starting to act like a bit of a military dictator. 'Now we **PROTECT STARKLEY AGAINST ANOTHER GRAVITYBURP!**'

What was going on with her?

She had a hammer in one hand and nails in the other. Everyone was a little worried she was just going to nail their shoes to the ground.

'Hamish,' said Dad, very seriously. 'You and your friends – come with me. It's time I explained something.'

5

Uh-oh!

Hamish's dad looked worried, as he led the **PDF** into the shed at the bottom of Elliot's garden – the official **WAR ROOM** Elliot had built just in case of scrapes like this one.

'Let me tell you my theory,' Hamish's dad said, pacing around, while outside the rest of the town got to work setting up anti-GravityBurp protection. 'Because, if I'm right about what's going on, Belasko is going to need all the help it can get. I'm going to need you guys to stay in Starkley.'

Buster puffed out his chest, proudly.

'And do what?' asked Hamish, eager for instructions.

'Just stay here,' said his dad. 'We'll work it out.'

Buster depuffed his chest. That didn't sound like much of a task. Hamish's heart sank, but he tried not to show it.

'As you know,' said his dad, 'it is vital to maintain the secrecy of **Belasko**. We have been fighting against our enemies for years now. There were **The Shrinkers**. There was **B.E.A.S.T.** You know all about the **WorldStoppers**. And, of course, you also know about **Axel Scarmarsh**.'

The **PDF** nodded.

Axel Scarmarsh had been the group's top enemy the last time the world had been in danger. Together with his awful inventions the Terribles, he'd tried to zap the world's biggest leaders and take over the planet. The last time they'd seen him, he'd been at the top of the Post Office Tower in London, just before it turned into a giant space rocket and shot off into the stars.

'For a while, we thought Scarmarsh was an evil genius who was pulling all the strings,' Hamish's dad continued. 'But then we found out he had a boss. Or rather – bosses.'

Hamish took a deep breath. He knew what his dad was about to say.

'There are a group of . . . "people",' said Dad. 'Called **"the Superiors"**.'

Everyone went, *Oooh*. That was quite an impressive name. But it was also a little unnerving. Nobody likes having superiors. Buster's mum was always complaining about hers.

'It's the Superiors who are doing this, I'm sure of it. They've been to blame for every strange thing that's ever happened here in Starkley. And now it looks like they're upping their game. They want to take the whole planet for their own.'

'But why?' asked Buster. 'What's wrong with their planet?'

Which is when Hamish's dad brought out a small device, no bigger than an orange, and placed it on the table in front of him.

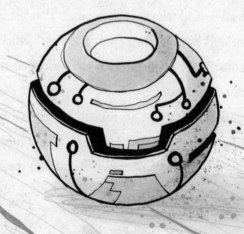

'What's that?' asked Venk.

Dad just smiled. Then looked at the device and said: 'Holonow – play.'

And something amazing happened.

A bright red light filled the room. It seemed to trace round the edges of the kids from the centre of the little metal orange, as if it was scanning them.

Then . . . blackness!

To Hamish's amazement, one by one, the room began to fill with stars! And satellites! And planets!

Planets that were the size of basketballs, but planets all the same.

A meteor whooshed through the room!

VOOOOOOOOOOOOOOOOM

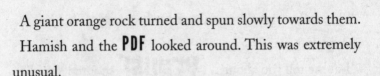

A giant orange rock turned and spun slowly towards them.

Hamish and the **PDF** looked around. This was extremely unusual.

It was like they were in SPACE!

'My name is Vapidia Sheen,' said a familiar-looking lady,

walking towards them across the night sky. 'Let me take you on a journey.'

Vapidia was one of the country's number-one celebrities. She was super smart but Scarmarsh had turned her into a blathering simpleton during his last attempt to take over the world – though, like everybody else, Vapidia had been returned to her normal brainy self, thanks to the **PDF**.

'She's a hologram,' explained Dad, quietly. 'This is all a hologram.'

'Let me tell you about ... **VENUS!**' shouted Vapidia.

The room began to twirl and turn, as if the shed was travelling at a thousand miles an hour.

The letters

V E N U S

spun past them.

The sound of a loud woman singing **'VEEEEEENUUUUUUUS!'** filled the air.

Clover was immediately sick in a bin.

'So the Superiors are from Venus?' asked Alice. Hamish's dad put his finger to his mouth, as suddenly, where Elliot's blackboard had been, a gargantuan grey planet came into view.

'No one really knows much about Venus,' said Vapidia, and Hamish half wondered if that meant they were just going to turn back again. (Although it seemed a long way to come just to hear that.) 'But Venus is almost the same size as Earth, and is often called our "sister" planet.'

It looked strangely beautiful, just hanging there, gently spinning. Hamish noticed that Elliot had gone quite red.

'Are you okay?' he asked.

'Holding my breath!' said Elliot quickly. 'You can't breathe in space – there's no atmosphere!'

'Venus is covered in thick cloud, which means no one has ever got a good look at it,' Vapidia continued as they seemed to get closer to the planet's surface and began to float through the clouds. Everyone had the unmistakable sensation of flying. 'Most of our space probes disappeared the second they landed on Venus. At one time, people thought it looked like a tropical paradise . . .'

Now the room transformed into a lovely tropical scene, with palm trees, and sunshine, and crystal-clear water lapping at their feet over wonderful white sands. Somewhere, someone strummed gentle guitar music and Hamish was sure he could smell his mum's caramel coconut suntan lotion.

'But now,' said Vapidia, 'we know that Venus has been

ravaged by THE LAVA OF A MILLION VOLCANOES!'

BOOOM!

The beach scene vanished as the room turned bright orange and smoke poured in. There was the sound of **EXPLOSIONS**, and there were **BRIGHT FLASHES**, and it **STANK OF BAD EGGS**, and it was just absolutely, horrifically **AWFUL**.

'VEEEEENUUUUUUUUUS!' sang that woman again.

'The planet is thick with smoke and fumes!' shouted Vapidia, as the children clung to one another. 'The throat-burgling, nose-assaulting pong of sulphur is everywhere! It is a heart-burningly, sweat-scarringly hot 470 degrees!'

There was a **ROAR** and the temperature seemed to **SOAR**.

'There used to be water here, but now there is NONE!' yelled Vapidia. 'And not one shop to speak of!'

'Okay, okay! We get it!' shouted Buster. 'Venus is rubbish! Turn it off!!!'

The kids had seen enough. Dad clicked off the Holonow and – just like that – they were back in Elliot's shed, staring at a little metal orange.

The kids slowly realised they were all still clinging to each other and gently moved apart as if it hadn't happened.

'Our experts at Belasko think the Superiors have had enough of how rubbish Venus is and want to get rid of us so they can take Earth over,' said Hamish's dad.

'Do you know,' said Clover, nodding, 'I absolutely don't blame them.'

'The gravity on Venus is less than it is here,' continued Hamish's dad. 'We think finally they have developed the evil technology to lift us all off the Earth, but they haven't found enough power yet. That's why they're using GravityBurps, and not . . . um . . .'

He struggled to find the right word.

'GravityBelches?' tried Elliot.

'Exactly!' said Hamish's dad. 'A GravityBelch would be catastrophic!'

So the Superiors were trying to build up to a GravityBelch. Right now, their GravityBurps were annoying but not all that dangerous. But a GravityBelch – that could spell serious trouble. They wanted a GravityBelch that would just go on and on and on – like your dad belching after a beer, or your auntie when her Sunday roast's all scoffed and she's got gravy down her top. They were building up to this belch with little burps. They were getting up a head of steam.

'But why a GravityBelch?' asked Alice. 'Where would it take us?'

'Venus!' Hamish guessed. 'Maybe they want to belch us all up to Venus. Make a straight planet swap. We wouldn't last five minutes on that rotten planet!'

'We'd have to bring shorts,' said Clover. 'It's hotter than Ibiza up there! And also there's the whole not being able to breathe thing.'

'Could they really belch us all the way to Venus, Dad?' asked Hamish.

'The Superiors are a superior breed of enemy. We need to be on our guard,' said his dad. 'Now more than ever. Thanks to the seeds.'

Yes. The seeds. There were still the seeds to worry about.

'But what are they, Dad?' asked Hamish, who to be honest until that moment had forgotten about the seeds because there was quite a lot of other stuff going on right now.

Hamish's dad looked like he was trying to figure out how to tell them something awful in the nicest way possible.

'They have been sowing the seeds,' he said, 'of an invasion.'

And then, from somewhere outside, came a noise.

6

Unusual Rumblings

UUUIUUUIUUUURRRRRRRRPPPPP!

Everyone in the town square screamed!

'Get inside!' yelled Madame Cous Cous, still brandishing her hammer. 'It's another GravityBuuuurp!'

Hamish and the **PDF** had done their best to help nail down anything that could be nailed down. Pictures were stapled to walls. Lamps were superglued to tables. Granddads were strapped to chairs.

All the town's dogs had had their leashes tied to the town clock, although that meant that now they were starting to float in the air together, like a really weird bunch of dog balloons!

This GravityBurp was stronger than the first one. If anything, it proved Hamish's dad's theory that the Superiors were most certainly building up to something. This was definitely going to be a job for the **PDF**!

Hamish and the gang burst out of
Elliot's shed the second they felt
the Burp and immediately began
to rise off the ground.

Around them, garden chairs
were levitating then shooting
into the air.

'Back in!' yelled Hamish. 'Get
back in the shed!'

'Whoooooa!' cried Buster,
who was floating up quickly.

Alice caught hold of him, bravely,
but now she too started to rise.

'I've got you!' yelled Clover, leaping
to grab onto Alice's shoelaces, but
now Clover started to levitate
as well!

Hamish's dad grabbed her, and the
other boys grabbed Hamish's dad.

'PULL ME IIIN!' yelled Buster,
his legs waggling over his head.

It looked like someone had invented
some kind of crazy Buster kite.

With a hard yank, Hamish's dad pulled everybody into the shed and slammed the door.

As they glided up to the ceiling, they were prodded and poked by Elliot's pencils, toy soldiers and microscopes that floated in the air around them.

'We've just got to ride it out,' said Hamish's dad, not knowing that just a few hundred metres away, in the middle of town, blind panic was taking over.

Some people had left their vacuum cleaners outside, and now the sky was full of them, whizzing past citizens stuck in trees.

Frau Fussbundler had both legs wrapped round a tree branch, and was hanging onto Mr Longblather's ankles.

Mr Longblather was holding onto Mr Slackjaw's ankles.

Mr Slackjaw was holding onto stinky Grenville Bile's ankles.

Grenville Bile was holding onto his mum who was holding onto the strange little man from the corner shop who wore a sailor's hat and he was holding onto old Mr Neate who was holding onto a dog who was holding onto a bone, sitting on which was a fly.

Anyone who saw them would have thought they were most probably doing some kind of skydiving display, except they were all screaming and shouting, *'Don't let go! Don't let go!'*

The dog didn't look that bothered, though.

Back in the shed, Elliot yelled, **'Aaaargh!'**, as he spotted dozens of sharp pins from his noticeboard rising up towards him, but thankfully Alice saw them too and blew them off course with a mighty puff. They lodged themselves in the ceiling around Elliot, in what looked for all the world like a low-budget circus knife-throwing act.

'This is a nightmare!' cried Buster, swiping a stapler that was headed towards him out of the way. 'You'd think it would be cool having no gravity, but it's actually incredibly inconvenient!'

And then ...

CRASH.

BASH. **THUMP.**

OW! **OOOOOF!**

It was over.

Creeping outside, watching vacuum cleaners fall to Earth, Hamish's dad made a decision.

'Okay, I need to get to Belasko,' he said, rummaging around in his pocket for his car keys. 'I have to warn them. The

Superiors are building up to something pretty spectacular. And I need to ask special permission to press the red button.'

'But . . . but can I come with you?' asked Hamish, hopefully. 'And what's the red button?'

'No,' Dad replied. 'You stay here. Go indoors where it's safe. Wear a helmet. Listen to Mum.'

'When will you be back?' Hamish asked, desperately. He was a brave kid – he'd proved that much – but he was much braver with his dad next to him.

'Stay strong, Hamish,' said his dad. 'And stay here. You kids know Starkley better than anyone. Well, you know most of it.'

What did that mean?

'Stay in town! And keep an eye on The Explorer!'

Hamish looked down at his watch – The Explorer. His dad had given it to him just before he'd left to fight evil the last time. Hamish felt desperately sad and worried, what if his dad didn't come back?

His dad knew what Hamish was thinking. He knelt down to look him in the eye.

'I'll be back,' he said, ruffling Hamish's hair. 'Keep a watch of the watch.'

And, with that, he jogged off to find his car, quietly hoping it hadn't floated away and landed in a pond somewhere.

'Right, you heard my dad, **PDF** – we need to protect the town!' said Hamish, doing his best to focus. The truth was, they all knew his dad hadn't said to protect the town. He'd just said '*stay*' in town. Hamish was secretly a little disappointed and annoyed his dad didn't think he could do something more useful than keeping an eye on things. He'd already saved the world twice! But he didn't want to make his dad cross by causing a fuss, so instead he decided to make the best of it and prove that his dad could trust him to help. 'First of all, we need a Burp Protection Plan.'

That was a sentence he'd never said before.

'Yeah,' said Venk, 'but, if they're getting more powerful and building up to a Belch, what can we possibly do?'

'Well, ultimately, we need to stop them altogether,' said Elliot. 'But, until then, Hamish is right. We need some kind of protection.'

'We need heavy boots,' said Alice. 'We need to fill our bags with rocks.'

Hamish nodded as she talked, but actually he'd stopped listening, because, as he'd watched his dad jog off, he'd noticed something.

'Also,' said Alice, warming to the subject, 'we need to put

things all over town we can grab hold of. Things on the side
of buildings that people can just hang onto if they start to
go up in the air.'

Hamish walked a little further through Elliot's garden as
Alice kept going. He stooped down. What was that? Had
that been there before? Surely it must have?

'And we should put whacking great nets up over the whole
of Starkley!' said Alice, oblivious to Hamish and pointing
her finger importantly, 'to stop us floating away into the
ether!'

'Hey,' said Venk, seeing that Hamish was now concentrating
on something else entirely. 'What are you looking at, H?'

Hamish prodded it with one finger.

It was a small green shoot.

It seemed that something had started to grow from one of
the seeds that they'd missed in Operation De-seeding.

The question was: what?

7

Mew What?

Hamish had dug up the little green shoot and put it in a small Tupperware box along with some soil. He didn't know whether to water it, because what if it turned out to be something nasty? But he didn't want to throw it away either, because that felt somehow cruel.

No, throwing it away would feel bad.

It was a living thing, even if it didn't talk or have thoughts or play Boggle.

Hamish decided the best thing to do would be to take the shoot home and study it. If he could keep an eye on it, it might help him to work out what the Superiors were up to. It was a clue, and a clue that he'd found.

He felt sad as he remembered again that his dad had already got in his car and left. It had seemed like they were on an adventure together, but that now he'd gone off to work with the grown-ups and the real agents. Hamish understood, but still . . . it made him feel a bit small and rubbish and useless, just when he'd started to convince himself he was big and not rubbish and useful.

'Hi, Mum,' he said, walking through the front door.

'Dad said you were in Elliot's shed when the last one happened,' she said, trying desperately to smooth down her hair, which seemed much more affected by these GravityBurps than anyone else's. 'I want you to stay in from now on. I got Jimmy to hammer some mattresses to the ceiling of your room so that if it happens when you're in bed at least you'll have a soft landing.'

Mum seemed stressed. She worked at Starkley Town Council, dealing with complaints, and there had been plenty today to keep her busy.

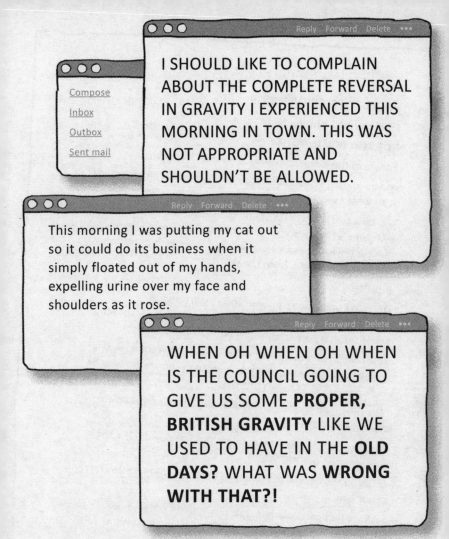

I SHOULD LIKE TO COMPLAIN ABOUT THE COMPLETE REVERSAL IN GRAVITY I EXPERIENCED THIS MORNING IN TOWN. THIS WAS NOT APPROPRIATE AND SHOULDN'T BE ALLOWED.

This morning I was putting my cat out so it could do its business when it simply floated out of my hands, expelling urine over my face and shoulders as it rose.

WHEN OH WHEN OH WHEN IS THE COUNCIL GOING TO GIVE US SOME **PROPER, BRITISH GRAVITY** LIKE WE USED TO HAVE IN THE **OLD DAYS?** WHAT WAS **WRONG WITH THAT?!**

But it was the piece of paper in her hand that seemed to be causing her the most stress.

'What is it, Mum?' asked Hamish, and she showed him.

It was an email.

PUBLIC OFFICE OF PRIDE

From the desk of Goonhilda Swag

NOT VERY POLITE NOTICE

People of the 'town' currently known as Starkley,

As you know, I visited you today and was not at all impressed with what I saw.

Old men stuck in trees! Cars on their roofs! Litter everywhere! You were so determined that I should have a terrible time that you even organised some kind of eclipse and made seeds rain from the sky!

RUDE!

Of course you made up some vulgar story about 'GravityBurps', but I am too smart and other words meaning smart for that sort of bunkum, claptrap and ballyhoo!

This is a formal notice that not only will I be recommending you are NOT given royal status, but that soon we will also be hiding you from view ALTOGETHER.

You will be off the maps. We will take all your signs down. You will be NOTHING.

Think yourself lucky. I recently visited Tramley-on-Sea and renamed it SOPPING WET.

I forced the people of Brannigan to rename their town LITTLE PLOPPING.

What I find particularly suspicious is that I can find no evidence of your town even existing before 1982. WHAT ARE YOU UP TO?

Soon I will return for a SURPRISE INSPECTION. If things aren't VERY DIFFERENT when I arrive to make my SURPRISE REPORT, then it's curtains for Starkley!

Warm regards, etc. etc.

Goonhilda Swag

'What does she mean she can't find anything about Starkley before 1982?' asked Hamish, who because he was only ten had never even heard of the year 1982 before.

'I don't know, but if we're not a proper town imagine how many complaints the council will get then!' Hamish's mum said, shaking her head. 'And, if we're not a proper town, then why would we even have a council? I'll be out of a job! Starkley will be off the maps! And everyone will move away!'

Hamish hadn't thought about that. Poor Mum. And where would they go? As boring as Starkley was – and remember it was the fourth most boring town in Britain – it was home. And, though home might seem boring sometimes, it's where you love the most. It's where you're loved the most.

Mum immediately felt the need for an emergency Mustn'tgrumble biscuit to soothe her stress levels and Hamish padded upstairs with his tiny green shoot in its box.

He put it by the window then sat down on his bed to stare at it.

What's going on this time? he wondered. *And when will Dad be back? What am I supposed to do now?*

And then the little green shoot seemed to move ever so slightly.

It was probably just the wind.

Hamish walked to the window to make sure it was shut.

But as he got closer . . . was that a tiny noise the shoot just made?

No. Can't be. Plants can't do that.

And then . . .

mew

Just that. As tiny a noise as Hamish had ever heard. Tinier than the noise an ant makes when it stubs its toe.

But a noise nonetheless.

The Gravity of
the Situation

The next morning, Hamish was woken rudely from his sleep by a familiar voice.

'ALWAYS BE PREPARED!'

He opened his eyes, startled, to find Alice's face just centimetres from his own.

She was frowning with her bottom lip out, like she just couldn't believe Hamish had the temerity to be so lazily asleep, in his own bed, in his own room, in his own house, first thing in the morning and before his alarm had even gone off.

'I've been up half the night filling people's boots with rocks to try and stop them floating off!' she said, hands on hips. 'Elliot and I drew up an Anti-GravityBurp plan and we all got to work! I do hope you feel rested, though, Hamish?'

Hamish felt immediately guilty. He hadn't even slept that

well, to tell the truth. He'd gone to bed early, because he felt a bit overwhelmed. He was worried about GravityBurps. He was worried about that small shoot, which still sat there by his window. He was worried about his dad having to go away again. And he was worried about his mum and her job.

And now he had Alice to deal with.

'Get dressed!' she said. 'Your mum's making breakfast and we've got school. And at lunchtime there's a special **PDF** meeting to discuss strategies and preparations! Unless you can't make it because you'd rather have sleepytimes?'

Hamish blushed. He was proud of Alice and the **PDF** for getting started on some plans, and she knew it.

Here's what they'd done:

- Put up some strongly worded notices reminding people about GravityBurps.
- Attached small hooks to the sides of buildings so people could grab on if they needed to.
- Put an old fishing net over the whole of the town square to stop people underneath it floating away.

Plus, lots of people had gone even further:

- Mr Slackjaw had filled all the car tyres in Slackjaw's Motors with gravel to try and weigh them down. His cars now made a crunchy sound the whole time, but he said that wasn't all that different from how they usually sounded. Plus, the gravelly noise made the driver feel like they were driving through a grand country garden.

- Margarine Crinkle, the milk lady, had popped a stone in every bottle of milk. 'The stone is free!' she told everyone, delighted, but secretly she charged them an extra 30p.

- Grenville Bile had been a very good boy, and eaten fourteen cheeseburgers and a piece of broccoli so that he'd be properly weighted down. And that's true, apart from the bit about the broccoli, because yuck.

- Madame Cous Cous had taken a hammer and nailed down all the sweets in her International World of Treats. It hadn't worked too well with the Creme Eggs, but with the Polos it turned out just fine.

Alice looked delighted by all this. You could always rely on the people of Starkley to rise to a challenge – even if the challenge was 'rising'.

'Can I ask you something?' said Hamish, sitting up.

'Unless it's "what is completely and utterly the very quickest way for me to get ready and be useful?" then no,' said Alice. 'Get dressed.'

'Do plants make noises?' asked Hamish, ignoring her.

'Plants? Make noises?' said Alice. 'No. Why?'

Hamish glanced at the shoot on the windowsill and weighed up whether to tell her. Maybe he'd been mistaken. Or perhaps he was just hearing things. But what if it was important?

'I think that little green shoot over there went "mew" last night,' he said, shyly.

'"Mew"?' said Alice, scrunching up her nose. 'Why would it say "mew"?'

That was the good thing about Alice. She didn't immediately say, 'Impossible!' or make Hamish feel silly. She questioned things. But, crucially, she believed him.

'Hmm,' she said, cupping her ear and getting up close to the shoot. 'We need to be careful. These are space seeds, after all. I mean, they're probably harmless, but who knows what they can do? You can't underestimate vegetation. Sometimes my mum puts fennel on pizzas and that absolutely ruins them.'

She pulled a nut and pickle baguette out of her combat shorts and pointed it at him, like a sword.

'Now **GET DRESSED.**'

At Winterbourne School, everyone was weirdly excited about the GravityBurps.

One kid – Puny Curdle – said her parents were going to turn a massive bouncy castle upside down and hang it over their garden, so the next time they all flew into the air they'd just bounce straight back down again.

Poor Robin had just got a new football and had gone outside to try it out. He'd only given it one kick when the GravityBurp started and it flew off at 200 miles an hour.

Astrid Carruthers said she'd been in the garden on her trampoline during the last one, and had ended up going so high she could see the Great Wall of China, but everyone agreed that what she'd probably seen was a big poster advertising fences outside the DIY shop.

Tommy Shunt had been in Juggling Class when all the balls suddenly blasted off into space, so they had to do stamp collecting instead. Lily Wax said all that happened in her house was that her dad's belly lifted slightly. Manjit Singhdaliwal had been competing in an under-elevens high-jumping competition at the time and had inadvertently broken all national and world athletic records. He was going to be on the news later because a big sports shoe company in America wanted to sponsor him.

Lots of kids seemed to think all this was brilliant fun. Only Hamish and the **PDF** seemed to grasp the gravity of the situation.

'I've been doing some thinking,' said Elliot in the playground at lunchtime.

While all the other kids played, the **PDF** had found a quiet corner and set to work.

Elliot had brought with him a small blackboard on wheels. It had a blue velvet curtain on the front. 'We know there are **GravityBurps**, and we suspect there are **GravityBelches**. But what else might there be?'

He pulled two short strings and the curtain parted to reveal his workings-out.

The kids all stared at the words. None of them seemed particularly terrifying. But then who'd have thought a burp could cause such chaos?

THINGS WE
DON'T WANT
by Elliot
GravitySneezes!
GravityHiccups!
GravityCoughs!
GravityFarts!

'What's a GravitySneeze?' asked Buster.

'Good question!' said Elliot. 'I assume it would be a great big **WHOOSH**.'

'A whoosh?' asked Alice, who'd convinced her parents to let her transfer to Winterbourne School from her old one nearby, just in case the world needed more quick thinking from the **PDF**.

(Well, to be honest, she hadn't actually convinced her parents to let her transfer. She just started turning up at Winterbourne instead, and no one dared argue with her.)

'Yes, a **whoosh**,' said Elliot. 'Like a powerful sneeze. Gravity would go side-on, and push you hundreds of metres along the Earth until, before you knew it, you'd end up in Siberia or halfway across the sea!'

'That's not good,' said Hamish. 'What about a GravityHiccup?'

'I suppose it would be a series of unpredictable tiny jumps!'

'A GravityCough?' asked Venk.

'Like a hiccup but quicker and more powerful!' said Elliot. 'The kind of thing that would launch you right over tall buildings!'

Everyone stared at the last one on the board. No one wanted to read it out loud.

'And . . . um . . .' said Buster. 'The last one?'

'A **GravityFart**?' said Elliot, matter-of-fartly. 'Well, I suppose it depends. It could be a little squeaker. You might not even notice it. It might be short. It might be long. It might go **PAAARP!** or **PFFFF!** or **DiNG-DiNG!**'

'Ding-ding?!' said Clover, a little worried about Elliot's bodily functions now.

'Or it might . . .' began Elliot, and the **PDF** braced themselves for whatever dark horrors Elliot was about to reveal, '. . . be silent but violent!'

The kids shuddered. That was the last thing they wanted. At least with a GravityBurp they could hear the **UUUUURRRRRP.**

'Just to be clear,' said Elliot. 'None of these things might happen.'

'Good!' yelled Buster. 'They're disgusting!'

'But we should be aware that they are possibilities. Who knows what dreadful technology the Superiors are harnessing?' said Elliot.

'He's right,' said Alice. 'Always be prepared.'

'Anyway, there are lots more,' said Elliot. 'I could go through them if you'd like?'

'No, don't worry, Elliot,' said Alice. 'I think we've heard enough.'

'**GravityVomits!**' said Elliot, not listening. '**GravitySweats!**'

'Okay,' said Hamish, trying to move things along.

'**GravityPees!**' yelled Elliot, quite lost in his own thoughts. 'Or a sort of gravity thing that spits snot everywhere when you laugh. I don't know what the word for that would be.'

'Honestly, don't worry,' said Venk, feeling queasy. 'We get the idea. Hamish, what do we do next?'

But, once again, Hamish had been distracted by something else and moved away from the group. In a crack on the concrete, he'd spotted something.

'Another green shoot,' he said. Something about this just did not feel right. They were all concentrating on the Burps and how to solve them, but these seeds had arrived for a reason. They were growing for a reason. An invasion, his dad had said.

'There's another one on the school roof,' said Venk, pointing upwards. You could just about make it out – like a small bright green finger finding its way through the tiles so it could wriggle towards the sunlight.

'This could be a problem,' said Hamish.

UUUURRRRPPPP!

All the kids in the playground rose up into the air for a second then landed back on their feet.

The sound of delighted giggling filled the air.

UUUUURRRRPPP!

Up they went again, maybe one or two metres, and down

they came again.

'This is **BRILLIANT!**' yelled Grenville Bile, but only because he knew it meant he wasn't heavy enough and could have more cheeseburgers.

UUUUUURRRRRPPP!

These were short Burps – tiny ones.

'They seem to be losing power, not gaining it!' said Alice, delighted. 'The Superiors must be giving up! Maybe your dad and Belasko have come up with a plan!'

The school bell rang and Mr Longblather flung open the doors. His moustache was nearly vertical and he had tomato soup all over his face. He'd obviously been halfway through a Cup-a-Soup when the world started burping.

'Everybody inside **NOW!**' he yelled.

Another tiny **BUUUUUUUUURRRrrrrP.**

Mr Longblather bopped his head on the doorway. Everyone rose slightly again as they began to run indoors.

Only Hamish stayed where he was.

Because he was watching the shoot.

And what he saw scared him.

Once You Pop

The rest of the afternoon passed without much incident.

Well, not exactly.

There were plenty more tiny GravityBu**JUUUUURRRR**ps and, even though Mr Longblather looked very sweaty and nervous, he explained that this was nothing to worry about.

After an earthquake, he said, it was 'quite normal' for there to be lots of little tremors. It was just nature's way of calming down, he said, so why shouldn't it be the same with whatever this was?

Mind you, he said all this while constantly slamming his head on the ceiling, or losing control of his whiteboard rubber, or watching Sharpies fly into the air and then land in his coffee. None of that seemed 'quite normal'.

But you knew when a GravityBurp was brewing because the first thing to rise was Mr Longblather's tie. It was like a polyester Early Warning System.

The kids were having a ball. As a precaution, the school had installed seat belts at every desk, but every time there was a Burp they all flung paper balls in the air to see who could get one in the wastepaper basket at the end of the room. Only Hamish wasn't joining in. He hadn't had a chance to explain his theory to Alice before they'd all rushed away, but now Hamish had a pretty good idea of what linked the seeds and the Burps and they'd arranged to meet after school to come up with a plan.

The bell rang and the kids of Winterbourne School streamed out of the gates, leaping and jumping, hoping to catch another GravityBurp, the way surfers hope to catch a big wave.

Alice was waiting at the gates for Hamish, as the rest of

the kids all disappeared off to the safety of their homes.

'What's the matter with you?' she said, seeing Hamish's serious face. 'Look, your dad'll be back soon. He's just gone to meet with Belasko. It's probably because of him that the Burps are losing their power.'

'Yeah, maybe,' said Hamish, as they walked towards the town square. 'It's just that I think I may have worked something out.'

Hamish noticed the hooks that people had been hanging on the side of houses, and the great big net above the town square. The grown-ups weren't enjoying the GravityBurps as much as the kids – the same way they get all huffy when it starts snowing, even though snow is pretty much the best thing ever, and if they had a brain in their body they'd all take the day off work and stop complaining. Kids had been ordered by the council to stay inside after school, as if after-school Burps might be worse somehow.

'Tell me then,' said Alice.

But Hamish didn't need to. Alice was about to see it for herself.

'Oh . . . my . . . gosh!' said Alice, her eyes for just a moment as huge and round as monster-truck wheels.

It was true. Hamish had been right.

All over Starkley, plant shoots no bigger and wider than a ruler had started to appear from the ground, stiff and emerald green.

There was a shoot poking over the top of a bin. There were shoots in Madame Cous Cous's gutters. There were shoots coming out of the drains. There were some shoots on the grass, and a single sturdy shoot edging over the top of old Mr Neate's chimney.

'All the seeds we missed,' said Alice, in awe, stepping backwards slightly.

'The GravityBurps pulled them up,' Hamish said. 'They've helped grow them!'

This is precisely what Hamish had been worrying about. Once, in the school library, he'd read something about how seeds grow differently in space.

Why?

Gravity.

Plant roots grow in the direction of gravity. But maybe the Superiors were using gravity to stretch the plants up quicker – to pull them up like socks – to get them to grow much faster than normal!

UUUUUUUURRRRRRRRRP!

Hamish and Alice shot into the air for a second, then landed back where they'd started. Their shoes smacked hard on the concrete.

All over town, dinner plates had lifted off tables and smashed back down again. Hats had flown off coat racks and landed on babies' heads.

UUUUUUUURRRRRRRRRRP!

'Another one!' yelled Alice. This one was stronger still, as once more they flew up into the air and slapped back down.

'Look!' yelled Hamish, as another short, sharp **UUUUUURRRRRP!** sent them skywards again.

Alice saw it too. Every time there was a short GravityBurp, the shoots got slightly taller.

It made perfect sense. These Burps were shorter for a reason.

You know how if you get your sleeve stuck in a door, you might pull at it and nothing happens? What do you do next? You don't just keep pulling. You tug at it. You pull quickly.

'Quick,' said Alice, grabbing Hamish before the next sharp gravity tug.

They started to run, but another quick **UUUUUURRRRRRP!** meant the only place they were going was up.

'LOOK!' said Hamish, landing and pointing at the bin. An immense shoot was now vibrating, shaking, pulsating . . . It swayed back and forth and it had grown before their very eyes.

Now it was nearly a metre tall.

'Please say it's just a big leek!' said Alice, who looked so scared that she was in danger of having a big leak herself.

But this was no mere vegetable. If it had been, then Starkley would be about to win so many regional Grow-a-Big-Leek competitions that it would put Manjit Singhdaliwal's high-jump medal to shame. And what kind of an invasion plan would that be for the Superiors to hatch? What war has ever been won by planting oversize veg in your enemy's garden?

No – Hamish knew there must be more to it than that.

Then ...

POP!

'What the—' started Alice, but now she was drowned out by another **POP!**

POP!

POPPOP!

POPPOPPOPPOPPOP!

The tips of the leeks were exploding like party poppers, sending sharp slivers of green streaming into the air like ribbons. They flipped and turned in the air, landing on rooftops and getting caught up in the huge net above.

POP!

Hamish looked again at the leek in the bin.

But here's the thing, – and please do not be absolutely, totally, utterly PETRIFIED of this – but what he did not expect ...

Was for the leek to be looking straight back at him!

It had a wide, sweaty head.

Two beady black eyes, like a snake.

It had two little holes for nostrils.

And it had TEETH.

'It looks like a massive Venus flytrap!' yelled Alice, backing away.

But these were even worse.

These were Venus spytraps! Tall and terrifying and created by the Superiors to fight against Belasko agents!

'Run, Hamish!' cried Alice.

But Hamish's feet were stuck to the ground. He couldn't

move. He stared at the abominable, toothy plant, as he studied the small wisps of black smoke snortling out of its nostrils and disappearing into the air. Now it didn't sound like a mewing kitten: it sounded like a panting horse. Even though it was quite clearly disgusting, Hamish found something about this enormous flytrap strangely beautiful.

'Maybe they're friendly?' said Hamish, forgetting for a moment everything his dad had told him about the Superiors, about all his past adventures, about how he should trust his own instincts. 'Maybe it's peckish?'

'Hamish!' cried Alice. 'What are you doing?'

'It's come such a long way,' said Hamish, his eyes wide, feeling in his pockets for a Chomp, his feet slowly starting to move towards the snarling green beast. 'I think it's just hungry.'

'Oh, it's hungry all right,' said Alice, pointing at the foamy slather that was now pouring from the plant's mouth . . . because that was a mouth, wasn't it? When she was younger, her cousin had given her a tiny Venus flytrap, and she'd watched it on the kitchen table as it opened its whole head to see what it could catch. These nasty nibblers moved slowly, deliberately, enticing their prey in. They were awful, evil, murderous things! No good could come from feeding one!

'Hamish, it's trying to tempt you closer!' she said, as another POP! sounded from a rooftop somewhere behind her and another ghastly, grizzly plant burst to life. 'Your dad was right! This is an invasion!'

Somewhere, someone opened a door, took one look at what was outside, screamed and slammed it shut again.

Alice looked across town. There were dozens of these dreadful things shaking their heads and opening their eyes and testing out their gnarly gnashers.

CLACK-CLACK-CLACK went one, straining at its roots as it snapped its teeth at the world, sniffing around, trying to find its lunch. **CLACK-CLACK-CLACK!**

Hamish was close now. He'd found a Chomp. He unwrapped it and held it out, with great uncertainty.

The plant seemed almost to smile at Hamish.

He could see all its teeth. He could count them. So many. So white, and so shiny, and so sharp in that smile that seemed to keep broadening . . .

And broadening. Widening.

Revealing more teeth.

And then more!

Clack Attack!

Hamish's hand was trembling as he held up his Chomp.

The great green monster-plant was staring at him, curiously, moving its head side to side as if weighing him up. Black smoke wisped thick from its nostrils as it panted and growled. Its stalk seemed to crack and harden in front of him, turning from soft light green to something more like scales.

'HAMISH!' cried Alice again, who'd been backing away, but keeping an eye on her friend. What had come over him? Had he been hypnotised? Or was he just trying to see good where there definitely wasn't any?

All these thoughts raced through Alice's mind as she stepped backwards. So much so that she didn't realise she had just come extremely close to a spytrap in a drain!

'HAAAAAMIIIIIIISSSH!' she yelled,

rising into the air.

But this time she wasn't rising because of a GravityBurp. The spytrap had CLAMPED onto her backpack with a CHAMP and was now shaking her around like a ragdoll.

Up she went!

Down she went!

Side to side she went, her boots clipping the branches of trees as she flew about.

And still Hamish stared at the beast in the bin.

'I AM NOT ENJOYING THIS ONE BIT!' yelled Alice, trying to kick at the spytrap behind her. **'HAMISH! SNAP OUT OF IT!'**

But Hamish didn't respond, innocently holding out his Chomp, moving closer and closer to the spytrap. It bowed its head, willing him, enticing him.

Thinking fast, Alice held both arms out straight above her head, and the next time the putrid plant yanked her angrily upwards she slid out of her backpack straps and landed hard on the ground. The spytrap started to gobble and chunk her backpack down, hungrily ripping it to shreds as she stumbled into the road and very nearly into the path of . . .

VROOOOOOOOOM!

'Get in!' yelled Buster, skidding to a halt in front of them in his mum's souped-up ice-cream van – the official vehicle of the **PDF**. As soon as he'd noticed these crazed carnivores, he'd known he'd better take a quick sweep around town in case anyone was in trouble. He beeped his horn and kept beeping it.

The noise seemed to break whatever spell Hamish was under.

Now he saw the spytrap for what it was.

ENORMOUS.

SWEATY.

FEARSOME.

TOOTHSOME.

And

HUNGRY!

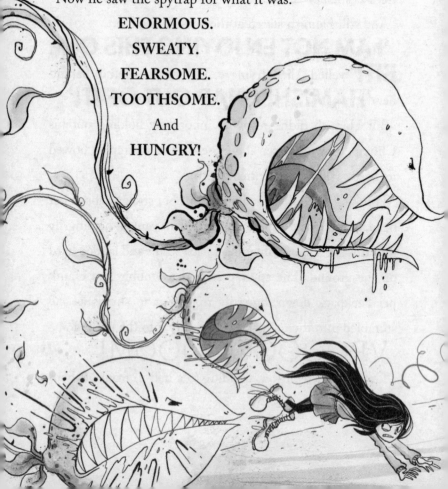

Hamish yelped and tossed his chocolate bar into the air. The oversized olive ogre swooped its neck and snapped the Chomp to pieces with its teeth as it fell.

It lunged for Hamish, **SNAP-SNAP-SNAPPING** its massive mouth mere centimetres from his face. Hamish panicked, jogging backwards. Buster had already turned the van around and was keeping an eye on his friend in the rear-view mirror. Alice had scrambled up through the window normally used for selling choc ices and kicked the back door open, now grabbing Hamish by his bag and dragging him on board.

'GO!' she shouted, and Buster needed no more encouragement than that. He jammed down the accelerator, the wheels spun on the concrete and off they sped!

'What has HAPPENED to Starkley?' said Hamish, red and sweaty and pressed up against the window as the van roared off. 'Why are these things here?'

Hamish knew he had to get to the bottom of this. If the Superiors were planning on sucking everybody straight into space, why even bother sending these awful attack-plants?

Everywhere he looked, more had stretched out from their seeds. **POP!** went one in a garden, and soil and gunk spattered everywhere. All these things needed was somewhere to grow. Somewhere their awful sharp roots could latch onto, like staples in paper. In shops. On concrete. Outside houses. Hamish caught sight of Frau Fussbundler standing on her front lawn, using a rolling pin to thoroughly whack a spytrap in the head. It had grown out of her trouser turn-up! There's a turn-up for the book!

As they sped further down the road, Buster wrenched a sharp left down Alumroot Alley.

Up ahead, Grenville Bile was trapped! Cornered by a couple of spytraps who seemed to be fighting over who'd get first bite of his tasty-looking, cheeseburger-filled belly!

Thank goodness they'd managed to get rid of all those other seeds after they'd rained down. Can you imagine what they'd be up against if they hadn't sucked them all up and dumped them in the sea?

'Alice!' yelled Hamish, as a thought struck him. 'What's in the freezer?'

Alice knew exactly what he was thinking. It was a classic Hamish Ellerby move! She slid open the freezer and began flinging ice creams out of the window.

Choccie Chimps®!

LEMONADE
Lick-me-ups®!

Strawberry Saddlebags®!

Grenville immediately picked one up and shouted, 'Thanks for the ice cream, but I think it might be more important to deal with these monsters!'

'They're not for you, Grenville!' yelled Hamish.

The spytraps began to sniff and salivate, with great gobby foam spilling from their slathery mouths. A flume of spittle arced through the air as one of them stretched towards the ice creams on the ground. It landed on poor Grenville, thoroughly sliming him. He tried to run for the van, but could only manage a slow, gooey jog before clambering in.

Buster hit reverse, spinning the van around and heading in a different direction. The late afternoon sun spread long shadows all over the streets – awful, snapping shadows. Some of the spytraps had grown giant leaves that now rose upwards and made them seem bigger and more monstrous still.

'What do we do, Hamish?' said Buster, skidding round another corner and narrowly avoiding the **SNAP-SNAP-SNAP** of another spytrap.

Hamish stared out of the window.

Old Mr Neate was wrestling with a spytrap.

A spytrap outside Slackjaw's Motors was tossing Vespas around.

Spytraps on roofs howled at the skies.

Buster had a point.

What do they do?

What should they do?

What *could* they do?

11

The Sweet
Shop Siege

Hamish had a plan.

'Buster – we need Madame Cous Cous!' he shouted, and Grenville, sliding the slippery, slurpery slime from his face, frowned.

'What's she going to do?' he said. 'Tell them off?'

But Alice understood. In their two close encounters with spytraps so far, there had been one thing that had helped.

'Hamish is right!' she said. 'Get us to **International World of Treats!**'

Buster span the van around and headed back towards the high street. He turned on his siren and flashing lights because this really felt like an emergency but also he just loved doing that.

They could see even more spytraps now, stretching and straining to munch on whatever they could – trees, bushes,

benches, Belgians. One spytrap had found a plank of old wood, and swallowed it whole, then burped and spat out a thousand tiny splinters.

And, to make things worse, even more of the thick green leeks had burst through soil or concrete, preparing to pop. A fresh wave! A second generation!

CLACK CLACK CLACK! went the spytraps as the ice-cream van rocketed past, each of them straining to reach into the road to stop them.

'Here we are!' yelled Buster, and they could see Madame Cous Cous outside her shop, wielding her big stick and trying to fend off a couple of snappity spytraps in the road.

'GET LOST!' she was yelling. Behind her, in the window of her shop, a dozen scared kids pressed their faces up against the glass. There was Venk and Elliot and Clover. There was Lola and Darcy, the twins from down the road. There was Finch Swift, Abigail Mess and Puny Curdle!

Buster skidded the van to a halt and Alice threw a couple of Vanilla Icebergs and a Peanut Mivvi into the road. The spytraps were distracted and angrily fought over them, while Hamish and the others jumped out and ran into the shop.

Madame Cous Cous followed, slamming the door shut behind them. She leaned against it, huffing and puffing, then realised something.

'There are only supposed to be **ONE-AND-A-QUARTER SCHOOLCHILDREN** in here at a time!' she bellowed.

'Madame Cous Cous,' said Hamish, politely, but meaning business. 'The only way to distract a violent beast is through food.'

'How **DARE** you!' said Grenville Bile, before realising Hamish didn't mean him.

'I gave one a Chomp and it went crazy. We rescued Grenville with a Lemonade Lick-me-up. We only managed to get in here thanks to a Peanut Mivvi and a couple of Vanilla Icebergs!'

'I think we need to feed them sweets,' said Hamish. 'Maybe they'll get tired and fall asleep.'

'Yes,' said Grenville, sarcastically. 'I find lots of sugar makes me sleepy too.'

'Okay,' said Hamish, as outside another spytrap **POPPED** into life and the shelves in the shop rattled and clattered. 'Maybe not sleepy, but distracted. And if they're distracted

we can work out what to do. Maybe we need to . . .'

He couldn't believe what he was about to say.

'Maybe we need to evacuate Starkley. Abandon it.'

Alice looked shocked.

'**WHAT?** Leave Starkley?' she said. 'Aren't you supposed to say . . . that we should fight? You're Hamish Ellerby!'

Hamish's face fell.

'That woman Goonhilda Swag wants to shut the whole town down anyway,' he said, sadly, as outside more **POP!**s thundered and rolled. 'She wants to take it off the maps and Mum seems to think she'll do it. Maybe we need to cut our losses.'

'Just because your dad's not here doesn't mean you can't do this, Hamish,' Alice said, gently. Hamish took a deep breath, how did Alice always know what he was thinking? 'Look at what we've already done, you and me and the rest of the **PDF**,' Alice went on. 'We don't need grown-ups to help us save the world! And we don't need their permission to either!'

While they'd been talking, they hadn't noticed Madame Cous Cous walking over to a doorway near the back of the room.

It was marked

DO **NOT** OPEN.

'But we don't know how to get rid of these things,' said Hamish, shaking his head and looking at his shoes. 'They're everywhere.'

'Hamish,' said Madame Cous Cous, thoughtfully. 'Did your dad ever mention **"THE BUTTON"**?'

'Yes,' said Hamish, frowning in confusion. How did she know about that?

'What exactly did he say?' Madame Cous Cous asked.

'He said something about talking to—' Alice began, stopping abruptly when Hamish elbowed her in the ribs. They were supposed to keep his dad's mission a secret.

'Has he gone to talk to **Belasko**?' suggested Madame Cous Cous.

The **PDF** all stared at the little old lady. What did she know about Belasko? As far as most people were concerned, Belasko was just a company that made all sorts of things. Matches. Bricks. Books that can identify the reader by touch alone.

'So the fight is on,' she said, mysteriously, and Hamish

noticed something about her had changed. She seemed taller somehow. More in control. Was there more to Madame Cous Cous than met the eye?

She straightened herself up, tossed her stick on the floor and pushed the door marked

DO NOT OPEN.

It slid to one side, revealing another door behind it, marked

DEFINITELY DO NOT OPEN.

She pushed open that door too and it also slid to one side, revealing yet another door marked

<u>YOU'RE MAD, YOU ARE.</u>

'Behind this door,' said Madame Cous Cous, getting ready to open it, as the children gathered round her, and as the shadows of the great Venus spytraps outside crept heavily across the floor of the shop towards them, 'is a very special and dangerous box indeed.'

What's in the Box?

Madame Cous Cous pressed on the door and with a great **KER-CHUFFF** of hydraulics and a **CHUNK-CHICK** of steel locks, it slid slowly away.

Inside was a room full of piles of old wooden boxes. On each one, in black stencil, were the words: **NORSKE SØTSAKER**.

In the middle of the room there was a plinth, and on that plinth sat a box that didn't look quite like the others.

'Is it the button?' asked Hamish, eagerly.

'It is not,' said Madame Cous Cous. 'It is something even more dangerous than that.'

The kids gathered round, nervously.

'Then what's inside that box?' asked Grenville, eyes wide.

Madame Cous Cous looked very serious.

'Many years ago, on one of my annual sweet-finding

missions,' she said, 'I found myself in the small port of Åyshøoderbroein.'

'Bless you,' said Grenville, thinking she'd sneezed.

'I was there to meet Erik and Viktor Viktorius – the greatest salesmen of Norwegian sweets and candy in the world.'

The kids all seemed very impressed as, I'm sure, are you.

'I was young and I was naïve. I was taken in by their top hats and twirly moustaches. One tall and bald with little glasses. The other much shorter and with a beret and monocle. I did not then understand the sheer power and force of . . . Norwegian confectionery.'

She shook her head, sadly.

'I bought many, many boxes of their candies. I have never sold one single sweet.'

'Why not?' asked Hamish.

'Because they are absolutely **DISGUSTING**,' she said, furious. 'Overwhelmingly, overpoweringly **HORRIBLE**. So bad that to this day I have banned **ALL NORWEGIANS** from my shop!'

'What's so horrible about the sweets?' asked Grenville, inching forward to try and open one of the boxes. Madame Cous Cous slapped his hand away.

'Oh, to Norwegians, nothing. They love them. But Norwegians are filled with Viking blood. They have the taste buds of bearded warriors. They didn't tell me that when they sold me their terrible wares, though, did they? But look!'

She flipped open a box by the wall.

'SALTED FISH BÅLLS!' she said, and the kids all took a step back as the fish stink stung their poor eyes.

She flipped open another. A bright yellow pong-cloud of dust wafted out.

'GOAT CHEESE GOBSTØPPERS!' she yelled, and the kids all shouted 'Eeeew!'

'And the worst of them all,' said Madame Cous Cous, back at the plinth, steeling herself for what was to come,

'SCANDI CANDGRENADES!'

She flipped open the box to reveal dozens of large, round, purple sweets.

'Cand grenades?' said Hamish, picking one up. It was the size of a cricket ball and terribly heavy.

'They're packed full of popping candy,' said Madame Cous Cous. 'Industrial strength popping candy! Very dangerous!'

Grenville looked delighted. He loved popping candy. He loved the way it seemed to trigger a thousand tiny explosions on your tongue. He loved creeping up behind his mum and opening his mouth by her ear so she could hear them all rattling away. He quickly grabbed one.

'Nonsense!' he said, shoving it in his great blathering gob.

'No, Grenville!' said Madame Cous Cous, aghast.

Grenville started to suck, and tried to chew, and with his mouth completely full attempted to say what sounded a lot like, 'Viking blood or no Viking blood, I'm sure I'll be fine!'

He tried to bite it in two.

'**Nnnngggggg!**' he said, his face bright red.

Something was cracking. It was either the Candgrenade or his tooth.

'NNNNNNGGGGGGG!!!'

Everyone held their breath as Grenville turned more purple than a Candgrenade. This great gobstopper was truly stopping his gob. But Grenville was stubborn. He had never been beaten by foodstuffs. Ever!

'NNNNNNNGGGGGGGG!'
CRACK!

He bit the thing in two and looked overjoyed.

POP! came a noise from somewhere in his cakehole. Then another tiny **POP!**

A moment passed.

POP!

'This isn't so bad!' said Grenville, chewing.

And then his eyes started to widen.

His brow began to bead with sweat.

His tummy started to rumble.

BANG!

Grenville looked startled.

He opened his mouth to speak and a great wisp of smoke puffed out.

Uh-oh! All the kids ran for the back of the room.

BANG! BANG! BANG!

'Oh my goodness!' yelled Grenville, hair now standing on end, feet leaving the ground with each bang. 'It packs quite the—'

BANG!

Grenville was juddering about now on his heels. He had the startled look of an electrocuted newt.

Thousands of tiny explosions were going off in his mouth. It sounded like the grand finale to a major fireworks display.

CHHHH! CHHHH! CHHHH!

BANG! BANG! BOOM!

He was spinning uncontrollably now, his tummy making the most disgusting noises. Every now and again, he rose into the air again slightly as a sharp gust of explosive wind shot from his rear end.

BANG! BOOM! BANG!

Poor Grenville!

'Make it stop!' he shrieked – **BANG!** – running around – **BANG!** – leaving a trail of smoke behind him. 'I've had enough!'

The kids all screamed, bashing into each other as they tried to run away from Grenville's strange and panicked bangs and booms.

But Alice nudged Hamish.

'Are you thinking what I'm thinking?' she said.

POFF! went Grenville's bottom.

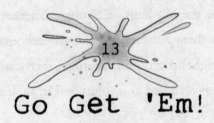

Go Get 'Em!

The two huge spytraps still stood guard outside the shop.

It seemed like the plants were continuing to evolve. Long, viney arms were unfurling from their sides menacingly. One of them curled itself round the doorknob and rattled it.

Inside, the kids were just as rattled. But the PDF had prepared everyone for action.

Anyone with a school tie had taken it off and wrapped it round their head.

Clover had licked two massive sticks of liquorice until they were so wet she could use them to draw warpaint under the eyes of every brave kid in the shop.

Elliot had put together a quick battle plan for them that utilised whatever they had around them.

Now they were ready for action . . .

First Alice kicked the front door open with her big army boots.

Then came the big bags of Siamese Sherbet. Lola and Darcy threw them hard against the ground outside so that they puffed right up in the air, creating a sort of smokescreen.

The spytraps coughed and spluttered in the thick, sugary clouds.

Then Finch Swift and Puny Curdle rolled two Candgrenades out into the street.

They trundled and bounced towards the enemy and came to rest at their roots.

Confused, the spytraps sniffed at the air and then lowered their heads to check out these little purple things.

The plants looked at each other, seemed almost to shrug, then licked them up and began cracking at them with their horrible, clackety teeth.

Quietly, Alice used Madame Cous Cous's stick to hook the door and quickly close it.

A second later . . .

BOOOOOOOOOM!!!!!!

The windows of the shop were spit-spat-splattered with awful green gunk.

There was a moment of silence.

The children all peeked through whatever small parts of the window weren't covered in plant slime.

'It worked!' said Hamish, amazed. 'Now we know how to get rid of these things!'

'May the world forever bless the noble Norwegians and their terrible treats!' said Madame Cous Cous.

'Right!' yelled Alice. 'To the van!'

The kids could taste victory.

Well, what they could actually taste were those awful Scandi Candgrenades. Grenville absolutely stank of them. He reeked. He was ponging up the air.

But victory was in the air too.

This would send a powerful message to those invisible Superiors: don't mess with the Starkley **PDF**! Hamish knew that Alice had been right about not giving up. He had to show his dad that he could cope with anything. That he could be trusted.

Every window in the ice-cream van was down. The lights were flashing and Madame Cous Cous was waving her stick out of the window, triumphantly. Buster had a stash of catapults in the glovebox and had handed them all out to anyone they passed. Now the **PDF** raced around town, firing Candgrenades up into the air, or flinging them into the open mouths of ravenous spytraps as they whizzed past.

BOOOM! went the one on top of Winterbourne School, flinging its filthy green goo everywhere.

BOOOM! went the ones by the town clock, and the ones outside The Queen's Leg.

Poor old Mr Neate was in his front garden, being tossed between one spytrap and another as they decided who'd get first nibble. That guy was having a terrible few days. Venk took aim with a catapult and lodged a Candgrenade straight into the open mouth of one of them. Clover shot one straight at the other. The popping candy set to work. It seemed even more powerful when it was in those nasty plants, with their acid juices and gloopy sap.

'I'm saved!' yelled old Mr Neate, delighted, and then he just stood there for a second, as a shower of gunk rained down on him.

On the van went, dispensing with every single spytrap in town.

'Never again will I criticise the proud Norwegian people!' yelled Madame Cous Cous, and, to prove it, she whipped out a Salted Fish Båll and popped it in her mouth.

BOOOOOOM! went the last spytrap they could see – one of the fresh batch that had struggled its way out of a crack in the pavement outside Lord of the Fries. The people inside cheered, triumphantly, then went back to munching on their battered sausages.

'Is that it?' asked Buster. 'Have we done it?'

'I think we have,' said Madame Cous Cous, looking queasy and stifling a fishy burp.

Buster rolled the van up to the town clock and put the hazard lights on.

The kids of Starkley clambered out and looked around.

No sign of spytraps. Anywhere!

'Invasion averted. So now what?' said Alice.

Hamish had a question of his own.

'Madame Cous Cous – earlier, when you mentioned this button,' he said, turning to the old lady who somehow didn't appear quite as old any more. 'What did you mean?'

Madame Cous Cous looked guilty, as if she'd revealed something she hadn't meant to.

'I think it's better you talk to your father about that,' she said. 'I shouldn't have said anything. I swore not to. When the time is right, he'll tell you about the button.'

'But—'

BVVVVVVT.

What was that?

BVVVVVVT.

Hamish felt something vibrating. He checked his wrist.

His dad's watch – The Explorer – was glowing green.

It was vibrating wildly now, like it was panicking. Hamish did not think this meant good news. Surely, by vanquishing the spytraps, they hadn't made things worse?!

Both hands suddenly shot round the watch face, pointing in one direction.

'Home,' said Hamish, worried. 'It's pointing towards my house!'

Forgotten Something, Hamish?

Leaping out of the van and running across his front lawn, Hamish had a good idea what he was looking for.

His dad was trying to send him a message from the front line of the battle against the Superiors. Maybe it was about this button thing. Maybe he was finally going to give Hamish something to do!

When he and the gang rocketed through the door of his dad's study, Hamish could see from the glowing edges of a closed drawer that something inside was flashing red.

Carefully, he slid open the drawer.

'The Holonow,' said Buster, peering in. 'Why's it flashing red?'

Hamish carefully took the machine out and placed it on the desk. Then, just like he'd seen his dad do in Elliot's shed, he pressed the single button on top.

VVVVVVVSHEW.

The room turned black.

The **Holonow** scanned the **PDF,** tracing around them with its lasers.

At first, all they could hear was noise.

Alarms.

Shouting.

Chaos.

Then the images flickered into life.

It looked like they were standing in front of a large, guarded building. Two enormous grey chimneys blew thick smoke into the sky above them. There was barbed wire, and towering gated fences, and sirens and barking dogs.

Now helicopters arrived, noisily chopping through the smoke, and men and women in black boiler suits flew through the air on ropes that cascaded down to the ground. Spotlights turned this way and that. Hamish could just about make out Belasko logos on the helmets of the people who now ran into the building.

'What's going on?' asked Venk, absolutely petrified.

A Vauxhall Vectra seemed to drive through the room, coming from behind them, and smashed through the gates and towards the entrance to the building.

It was Hamish's dad! He was there – wherever there was. He must be about to ask for Hamish's help!

'Port Fenland Nuclear Power Station,' said Vapidia Sheen's hologram, suddenly beside them, and very serious. 'The scene of an attempted burglary this afternoon.'

She kept appearing and disappearing, as if the message had been recorded in a hurry or in a room with a terrible phone signal.

'The Superiors,' said Elliot, looking terrified. 'They need power for their GravityBelch, don't they? Well, what's more powerful than nuclear energy?'

Next the room was filled by the sight of a giant yellow

ball, the size of a grown-up. It had metal rivets and black hazard signs. It rolled towards them like an enormous heavy boulder; they all held onto each other for courage.

'Beware the **NUCLEAR BALL!**' said a flickering Vapidia, as agents in uniform loaded it into a van. Then she and the van disappeared with the click of her fingers.

Now the scene shifted and it was like the kids were at sea. Monstrous waves crashed around them. The roar was deafening. There were great, craggy black rocks in the distance – the type that must have sunk a thousand ships. The whole room seemed to rise and fall as the kids swayed around, feeling seasick even though they all knew they were definitely still safe in 13 Lovelock Close. The damp in the air felt like it seeped right through them.

They shivered as another great wave rose and fell to reveal . . .

An island.

It was dark, with more black rocks and caves, and it was heavy with sinister black moss and wet, wilted trees. Tall, limp mushrooms and slick brown toadstools grew at its edges and, as they got closer, Vapidia flickered back and clicked her fingers.

The letters . . .

. . . spun through the room and settled in front of this most ghastly place.

'FRYKT,' Alice gasped, in shocked awe.

She knew of this place all too well. The last time they'd heard its name had been when they were fighting the evil Axel Scarmarsh. **FRYKT** was where the minion of the Superiors had done all his research. This was the small island on which Axel had developed his fearsome Terribles – the awful monsters he'd funnelled into Starkley to undertake their gruesome deeds. They'd lurched into town, as Hamish's friends and neighbours stood frozen in time, stealing grown-ups and leaving the place in utter chaos. **FRYKT** had been where Scarmarsh had lived when he was hatching his plans to zap the world's leaders using Otherearth and the Neverpeople. And, when they'd seen him off the last time, they'd never thought to check the place to see what else might be going on.

Now, as the projections from the **Holonow** made it look as if they were flying over the island, they could make out what appeared to be a concrete disc the size of an entire football pitch. And right in the centre of it was an enormous, twisted brass rope, anchored to the ground.

'What's that?' asked Buster, though he felt like he'd rather not know. 'What's that weird big rope?'

Now the image started to stutter and change.

Vapidia stared upwards. But at what?

Her face turned to horror.

What was she staring at?

Then came Dad's voice, breaking up, appearing and disappearing. He sounded strained and panicked!

'Hamish . . . go . . . FRYKT . . . DANGER!'

And then everything disappeared in the blink of an eye, as Hamish's mum walked into the room, flicked on the light switch and said, 'Anybody fancy a chocolate Mustn'tgrumble?'

H

'Okay, that was crazy,' said a very pale Elliot, as they all sat around Hamish's lounge.

The rest of the **PDF** looked as shaken as he did.

'What are we supposed to do with all that information?' said Clover, hoping the answer might be 'absolutely nothing'.

'Hamish's dad was telling us the Superiors are going to strike,' replied Alice.

'But how?' asked Buster. 'Belasko hid the Nuclear Ball, right? Or have the Superiors got their own? Is that all they need to do a GravityBelch?'

Hamish nodded to himself. 'I think the answer is on FRYKT,' he said.

'Sure,' said Venk. 'But what are we supposed to do about that? It's in the sea. I don't think many budget airlines fly there.'

'Mr Slackjaw has a tugboat,' said Alice, moving to sit next to Hamish. 'How hard can a tugboat be to sail? You just point it where you want to go and then get there, extraordinarily slowly.'

'We won't look like heroes in a tugboat,' said Venk, image-conscious even in times of epic danger.

'Do we even know where FRYKT is?' asked Clover, once again hoping the answer might be 'no, so let's not worry about it'.

Hamish held up **The Explorer**. The hands were still stiffly pointing in the same direction. No matter which way he turned the watch, the hands stayed rigidly pointing one way, like a compass pointing north. Earlier, Hamish had thought these hands had been pointing at 13 Lovelock Close. But no. They'd been pointing at the coast.

'I'm sure Mr Slackjaw won't mind us borrowing his boat,' said Hamish. 'It's a matter of life and death. I mean, Dad sent me a message, right? To say he really needs our help.'

The idea that his dad, so big and so brave, might need Hamish's help filled him with pride. But also fear.

'We should leave as soon as possible tomorrow,' he continued, hiding this fear from the others. 'We have to find out what's going on. We don't need to get too close, just take a look. But I'll understand if you don't all want to come. I mean, that place looked terrifying.'

The **PDF** took a collective deep breath and looked at each other and nodded.

'All for one,' said Elliot, and Venk agreed.

'Plus,' said Buster, 'I've got a little something up my sleeve. A new design I've been dying to try out.'

'Well, you're not going without me,' said Clover. 'After all, I've already got a half-spy, half-pirate costume. It would be nice if it actually came in handy for once.'

The gang high-fived.

'Good,' said Alice. 'Now let's all go home and try to get some rest.'

Hamish traipsed upstairs.

He knew he had to act. The message had made it clear that **FRYKT** was important and going to see it for themselves was the only way to work out what the Superiors' plan was and hopefully stop it. Everything would be so much easier if his dad was back. Still. His dad had given him a clue. And that clue was like a mission. It had to be the right thing to do.

He still felt silly he'd nearly given up. His dad wouldn't have and his message showed that he needed the **PDF**'s help!

As he brushed his teeth, Hamish wished he could tell his dad what he'd been up to. How they'd taken on the spytraps and won. How they'd rid the town of every single one of them. He knew his dad would be proud of him and that made Hamish feel better. It gave him confidence in what lay ahead. Sure, it would be dangerous, but it was just a reconnaissance mission. They were only going to have a look.

He finished brushing his teeth, wiped his mouth, and walked towards his bedroom door with the football stickers and the big 'H' on it.

Hamish was so focused on thinking about tomorrow and what lay ahead that he had completely forgotten that behind that very thin, plywood door something unspeakable was lying in wait.

Guest Who?

Hamish walked into his bedroom, turned to close the door, then spun back to look at the room.

Something was definitely not right here.

What the . . . ?

His 'I ♥ OCELOTS A LOT' duvet was on the floor.

His bedside lamp was missing its shade.

His life-sized Captain Beetlebottom model had lost its head.

The light bulb dangling from the ceiling was swaying from side to side.

And there were feathers everywhere!

Hamish stooped to pick one up. He stared at it and, as he stood back up again, he noticed the remains of his ocelot pillow nearby. It must have exploded!

As he moved, his carpet squelched underfoot. Yeuch! What was that stuff? It was slippery and green and looked

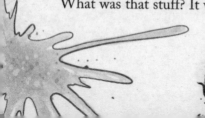

just like the slime he'd noticed coming from . . .

Uh-oh.

SSSCRAAAAWWWWWLLLLL!

The curtains billowed out towards him and out from between them loomed the giant face of a Venus spytrap!

Hamish jumped and yelped. He'd forgotten all about the one in his bedroom!

The plant was still rooted to the little plastic Tupperware container he'd potted it in, but was wiry and quick and reaching for him.

SNAP-SNAP-SNAP! went its jaws, weaving and bobbing towards him, and Hamish put up his hands to defend himself. Hamish fell to the floor, crawling backwards to avoid the creature's quick lunges. He felt behind him for a weapon, but all he could find was an old boxing glove Jimmy had left in there. He quickly shoved it on as the beast went **SNAP-SNAP-SNAP!** at him again.

Hamish managed to land one soft blow to the creature's face – **WHOFF!** – and knocked over his bedside table with a **CRASH** as he tried and failed to scrabble to his feet. Wait – there were Chomps in there! His secret night-time stash!

But he couldn't quite reach the drawer!

CLACK-CLACK-CLACK went the enormous plant, lunging for Hamish again, this time knocking books off his shelf and smashing his Xbox controller right against the wall.

'Will you **KEEP THE NOISE DOWN?'** yelled Jimmy, opening the door, and making a pompous face. 'These walls are **VERY THIN** and I am **TRYING** to Skype with my **GIRLFRIEND**, Felicity Gobb!'

'Jimmy!' yelled Hamish, pointing at the spytrap.

'It's **JAMES!'** screamed Jimmy, oblivious, and closing the door again so quickly that a hundred more feathers now danced around the room from the force.

CLACK-CLACK-CLACK! SNAP-SNAP-SNAP! Now the spytrap was really stretching and straining to get closer to Hamish.

The boy pushed himself as far back as he could, but he was almost up against the wall. One hand tried to swipe at the plant with his boxing glove, while the other felt desperately around on the floor beside him.

Where was the drawer? Where were the Chomps?!

The plant was right up to his face now, breathing and seething. There was nowhere left to run. Hamish squinted, back pressed flat against the wall, sweating and ready for whatever was about to happen. He could feel the hot, wet burn of breath from the creature's nostrils flaring on his face. He could smell its acid breath and it stung his eyes.

The beast stared at Hamish, and moved its great head around his, wondering what to start with. A nibble on the ear? A snap at the nose?

Hamish could hear Jimmy in the room next door, dully mumbling some dreadful poetry to Felicity Gobb.

If this is my last moment on Earth,
thought Hamish, I really don't want it to
be while listening to
Jimmy's soppy poetry.

And then the Venus
spytrap seemed to make
its decision.

It opened its mouth
and stretched its jaws
WIIIIIIDE open.
Hamish
could hear its
skin crackle
and pop.

Tiny green blisters exploded, spraying a fine mist of plant juice all over Hamish's hair.

And then, as his tummy sank and he closed his eyes, a thick red tongue flopped out and licked Hamish right up the face.

SCHLUUUUUUCK.

Hamish felt his nose being dragged upwards, then his eyebrows, then his forehead.

There was silence for a moment.

There was gunk everywhere.

The plant's head shot back, and Hamish and the spytrap stared at each other.

And then the plant roared '**EEEEEEEEEEWWWWWWWWW!**', shrieked and retreated, shocked.

It shook its head, and spittered and sputtered to rid itself of the taste of yucky Hamish Ellerby.

'**UCCCCHHHUCCCCCHHHHHUCCCCCHHHHH!**' It wiped its mouth with its lank, viney arms. And then it stared at Hamish, looking almost hurt that he'd decided to taste so bad.

Hamish didn't know what to do. So he just shrugged, apologetically.

In a way, he was a little offended that he seemed to taste so revolting. He'd had a shower only yesterday, and had even used some of Jimmy's Tropical Pumpkin Man Mist on his underarms.

The plant was still making those strange noises and looking befuddled. It didn't seem very dangerous now. Its eyes had softened, and it wasn't standing as tall as it had before. It looked beaten and annoyed, like it had been banking on eating Hamish and now it was back to square one, in a right old huff.

Well, Hamish had been raised always to be polite and try to put people at ease. So he looked at the floor, spotted a Chomp and, moving very slowly, he offered it to the spytrap.

The plant backed away. It didn't trust Hamish any more. Not since he'd dared taste so foul.

But Hamish persisted, unwrapping the Chomp and pretending to take a bite and saying, 'Mmmm!'

Now the spytrap, which must have been starving, moved a little closer – but like a wild dog, suspicious of Hamish's motives.

Then it sucked the Chomp from Hamish's hand and chewed it slowly . . .

Then quicker, devouring it in just two bites!

Its great tongue hung from its mouth and its eyes widened, asking for more.

'That's all I have,' said Hamish, feeling awkward again and like a very bad host. The plant growled a low, sad growl.

Mind you. Hamish did know where he could get some.

Sweetness
and Fight

'Are you **KIDDING** me?' said Madame Cous Cous, standing at the door of International World of Treats very early the next morning. 'We only just took care of these horrible things and now you want me to . . . take care of one?'

She looked disgusted.

'What am I supposed to do with it?'

'This one isn't like the others and he could be important,' said Hamish. 'For research! We might learn something about the Superiors! Alice always says things like: "Know your enemies!" and "Be prepared!". I've named him Vinnie. I'm pretty sure he's vegetarian so he's perfectly harmless. He just likes to lick people, like they're lollies.'

SCHLUUUUUUK.

Unfortunately, Madame Cous Cous's hair was not the type of hair that responded well to licking. The gunk on the spytrap's tongue was like hair gel, and Madame Cous Cous now looked like one of those weird troll dolls that are supposed to be cute, but instead give you nightmares.

'I am **NOT A LOLLY!**' yelled the old lady.

Hamish had tried to keep Vinnie fed all night, but the plant hadn't responded particularly well to any of the leftovers that Mum kept in the fridge. He hadn't liked her Duck à la Chocolate Orange. Nor her Extra Fiery Chilli Jam Lamb. Hamish hadn't wanted to tell his mum that he had a ravenous alien super-plant in his bedroom, so he just told her he was planning an enormous midnight feast and wasn't to be disturbed. She was still so distracted by the obnoxious emails she was getting from awful Goonhilda Swag, and the ever-growing complaints from the rest of Starkley about the battle with the spytraps, that she hadn't even noticed when Hamish got up early and wheeled the spytrap out of the house in his grandma's old tartan shopping basket.

'Vinnie likes Chomps,' said Hamish, as Madame Cous Cous shook her head and tried to do something with her hair. 'Maybe you'll finally be able to get rid of those Goat Cheese Gobstøppers. Just make sure you keep him away from the Candgrenades. We don't want to blow this one up!'

SCHLUUUUUK.

Now Hamish had troll hair too.

A piercing whistle made him spin around.

It was Alice. She was in full combat gear. Black shorts, black shirt and she'd dyed a bright yellow stripe through her hair. She looked like a walking hazard sign.

'Let's rock,' she said.

Down at the coast, as the waves crashed onto the cliffs, Hamish and Alice skipped down the steps to a small area of beach.

The kids knew it was important to visit **FRYKT**. The island must have something to do with whatever the Superiors were trying to do with the Nuclear Ball. Hamish was sure his dad must still be at Port Fenland Nuclear Power Station, defending it, which was why he couldn't get to **FRYKT** himself. Well, Hamish wouldn't let him down!

But what would he find, he wondered? What was at the end of the rope that the **Holonow** had showed them?

Buster was loading the tugboat and mopping his brow. Mr Slackjaw had said Hamish could have the boat for the whole day, on account of ridding Starkley of those spytraps.

It was nice to be appreciated.

Hamish looked at the boat. It didn't seem all that impressive. It had a white two-storey cabin with little

steps and a small yellow winch. There were fat black tyres all around the outside to stop it from bumping into things too hard. And it had a level platform at the back, onto which Buster was now dragging the team's mopeds. They hadn't needed them in a while and it was nice to see them again. Still, Hamish thought, that was a weird thing to bring.

'Um, Buster,' said Venk, voicing Hamish's thoughts, 'I'm not sure we'll be needing the mopeds at sea. On account of being . . . you know . . . at sea.'

'ALWAYS BE PREPARED!' cried Alice.

'Plus, Buster's made a few nautical adjustments.'

Buster looked proud but said nothing.

'Are we ready?' asked Clover, from the cabin. She had decided against the half-spy, half-pirate costume, because wearing dark glasses and an eyepatch made it very difficult to see, plus she'd never enjoyed hopping around on one leg. So she was dressed up in her best sea captain disguise. Her big fake beard was covered in cheese as she'd already eaten all her sandwiches for the day even though it was only about 7 a.m.

The rising sun cast an orange blush across the sea, as they all strapped on their life jackets. It looked peaceful out there. Sure, they'd have to be careful not to be spotted. And yes, they were going straight to an island which may or may not be owned by the most powerful beings in the universe. But as he looked around at his friends on the boat, a small part of Hamish felt like perhaps this adventure could be fun.

MM

'AAAAARRRRGGH!' yelled Elliot, clinging to the roof of the cabin. 'This is **NOT FUN!**'

About four miles outside Starkley, with the town not even a tiny dot on the horizon, the waves had begun to get really

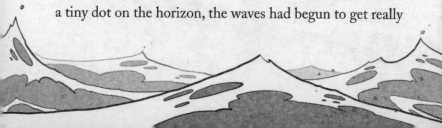

rather huge indeed.

The tugboat was made of very sturdy stuff, but the **PDF**? Not so much.

They seemed to have been sailing on these giant waves for ages. Well, not 'sailing' exactly. This was more like lurching.

'I think I see **FRYKT**,' said Venk, lying. 'Right, can we go home now?'

Up, up, up the tugboat went, in what felt like slow motion. Down, down, down it came again, its stern crashing into the next wave and splattering the front of the cabin window.

Clover had been sick a record four times so far. Maybe she shouldn't have had her lunch so early. Hamish remained with Buster by the wheel of the boat, staring intently at his watch to make sure they weren't being blown off course.

Up, up, up the boat went again, and then the heavens opened and the rain started. Real rain. Hard rain. The type of rain you feel in your bones. It was cold out at sea. The sun, which had looked so promising, seemed to have given up on the day.

'Um, did any of us actually tell our parents where we were going?' asked Venk, swaying around. 'Only now it seems like we probably should have.'

'Oh, sure,' said Alice, sarcastically. '"Hey, Mum, we're just

going to drive a tugboat into the sea to spy on an alien race who are trying to steal a nuclear reactor. Should be home about four.'"

And then, in the dim distance, Hamish spotted it.

Not the island.

No, no.

He went white in the blink of an eye.

'WHAT IS THAT?' yelled Venk.

'Is that . . . a boat?' asked Elliot, trying to defog the window. 'Or a lighthouse?'

'Is it an old fort?' tried Clover, hopefully, opening a side window, which just wet her face and made the rain far louder.

'No,' said Alice, her face darkening. 'No, I know what that is.'

The thing was solid. It was wide. It was hard. Seagulls landed on it, uncertainly. It was the height of a bus, and as the waves smashed and bashed at it, it did not move at all.

'It can't be,' said Hamish, shaking his head.

But it could. And it was.

'It's so green!' said Elliot. 'And . . . it's getting **BIGGER!**'

Elliot was right. This thing in the middle of the sea was growing. And, every time it gained another tiny millimetre in height, it GROANED.

This was the biggest Venus spytrap in the world.

Out here. In the sea.

This was BAD.

The kids screamed, Buster wrenched the steering wheel and the tugboat suddenly managed speeds no one would ever have thought it capable of.

A few miles away, the sun was brightening the waves ahead, and Buster began to slow the speed of the boat.

'I think it's our fault,' Hamish said.

'What is?' asked Alice.

'That thing. That enormous planty thing in the sea.'

'How can it be our fault?' asked Clover, wrinkling up her nose.

'When we swept all the seeds up,' said Hamish, 'Mr Slackjaw said the grown-ups were going to dump them all in the sea. The salt water must have carried them off and bound them all together. Maybe it made the seeds grow into that huge thing out there. Who knows what happens when you mix space stuff with Earth stuff?'

Standing in the rain outside the cabin, they all stared at the spytrap in the distance. Somehow it looked just as big as it did when they were much closer.

'We can't have a terrifying sixty-metre Venus spytrap in the sea off Starkley,' said Elliot, standing at the front of the boat. 'What would Goonhilda Swag think about that? I'm pretty sure it would definitely count against us, having a local sea monster.'

Poor Mum. A local sea monster would be all she needs, thought Hamish.

Buster turned off the engine so they could think.

As they drifted quietly further towards **FRYKT** – with Hamish's watch pointing the way as ever – Hamish didn't notice that the rain had completely stopped. It was only when he felt the sun on his face that he did.

'Hey,' he said. 'At least it's sunny.'

'What are you talking about?' yelled Clover. 'This is horrible weather!'

Hamish scrunched up his nose.

'It's glorious!' he said, turning around.

'It's dreadful!' shouted Clover, furious. 'Why are we even standing outside?'

Hamish looked at Clover properly. She was shivering, her beard long and soggy, her little arms up in the air trying to both fight off the rain and pull her sea captain's hat down. Fat raindrops thundered down all around her. But Hamish was standing in perfectly calm weather.

'How is that possible?' said Hamish, almost to himself.

At the front of the boat, it was like summer. At the back, a shivering Clover was getting battered by cold winds and fearful storms.

'Whoa!' said Buster, standing between them. He looked at Hamish in the sun. He looked at Clover in the rain. 'Clo, get over here with us!'

'It's like a weather force field,' said Elliot, as Clover stepped into the sunshine. 'One side rainy, one side sunny.' He clicked his fingers. 'That rain and those storms were put there, to keep people away!'

The Superiors!

That meant one thing.

'We must be close,' said Hamish.

'There!' yelled Venk, from the cabin above, with just a hint of trepidation in his voice. 'There it is!'

And at the end of a rainbow that started very colourfully, but grew darker and blacker as it dipped towards the horizon, was the fearful enemy island of **FRYKT**.

17

FRYKT!

Did you know that **FRYKT** is a Scandinavian word?

It means ...

FEAR.

None of the **PDF** spoke any Scandinavian languages. It wasn't really a main priority in Winterbourne School, any more than learning the History of Wood or Lemon Studies.

In many ways, this was lucky. Because had the **PDF** known they'd be taking a small tugboat to a place which is essentially called **'FEAR ISLAND'**, it is very likely indeed that they might have decided to do something else instead. Like anything else. Even Lemon Studies.

Hamish stared at the island. It looked even worse in real life than it had through the **Holonow**.

As the gang allowed their little boat to drift closer, furious waves crashed against sharp black rocks. Unfamiliar grey birds, with long tongues and cruel eyes, strutted by the shoreline, like watchmen overseeing the whoosh of the breaking tide. Cold water now sprayed in the air, carried on a sharp, bone-chilling wind that whistled around them, whipping Alice's hair and rocking the tug.

There didn't seem to be much in the way of trees. Or grass. Or bushes. There was almost no colour whatsoever. It was like looking at an old film. A fog hung low in the air, and the whole place felt weighed down by a misty grey ceiling.

'Maybe it's not so bad when you're actually on the island,' suggested Clover, eyebrows raised. 'Maybe there's a corner shop, or a lovely deli.'

She was trying to look on the bright side. But this seemed like a place that had no bright side. A place that was always dark. But in a way it reminded Hamish of the video they'd seen of Venus, covered in gases that hid the truth of what was really going on on the surface. Maybe Clover was on to something. Though it probably didn't have a deli.

'Hey, what do you mean, "when you're actually on the

island"?' said Venk, wiping sea spray from his sunnies. 'We're not going on the island, are we? I thought we were just taking a look from the water?'

'That was the plan, but ...?' said Alice, glancing at Hamish to see if what she was about to suggest was on his mind too.

'We can't see much from here. We should look around. I'll go,' said Hamish. 'Alice, will you please come with me?'

'Absolutely,' said Alice, determined, smiling at her brave friend.

Sometimes you can say brave things because you know it's the right thing to do. But even as they leave your mouth it's like you're hearing someone else say them. At least getting all the way to **FRYKT** to scope things out would impress Dad, decided Hamish, even though he was still a little apprehensive about this place. I mean – look at it.

'You guys stay here and keep the boat running,' said Hamish.

'But what if you bump into a Superior?' said Elliot. 'We don't know what they look like and if we don't know what they look like how will you know to avoid them?'

Elliot had a point. I mean, they knew who their enemies were by name. But they didn't know where they were, or what they looked like, or what they were capable of. They could be as big as a house. They might be able to leap whole buildings. Maybe they were invisible. Perhaps they'd look like toadstools, or enormous fanged mice, or like little green aliens from comics. What if they had big metal fists capable of crushing a little boy with the click of a big metal finger? What if they were just a big bunch of teeth scuttling around on some feet?

'That's exactly why we have to find out more,' said Alice. 'We need to know what we're up against if we're to save the world from whatever we're up against! And we need to know how to stop these GravityBurps!'

'One problem,' said Hamish, staring out at the stormy, choppy waters that stood between them and **FRYKT**. 'How do we get onto the island?'

Buster smiled.

'These are **AMAZING!**' said Alice, bouncing over a tall wave, feeling the spray on her face and grinning widely.

They certainly were. Buster had indeed made some adjustments to the **PDF**'s mopeds. He'd attached water skis to the bottom and created a sort of moped jet ski. A mo-ski!

156

'**Whooooaaaa!**' said Hamish, who was yet to find his sea legs, and was already completely soaked. He kept slipping and spinning the jet ski round in tiny little circles.

'Come on!' said Alice, revving hard, a plume of water rising in the air behind her.

As the two kids buzzed away from the tug, and their friends got smaller and smaller, a mist rolled across the waves in front of them.

They shot through it – **WHOOF!** – and began to slow.

Around the edges of **FRYKT**, a thin sheet of ice cracked and splintered on the water. The jet skis silently glided onto it, sending those strange birds flap-flap-flapping into the fog above. Hamish and Alice found themselves on dry land.

Well, actually moist black land with the look of freshly turned soil. But you know what I mean.

They climbed off the mopeds and their feet sank into the ground as they walked. It was like a different planet.

'Which way?' asked Alice, shivering. The temperature seemed to have plummeted as soon as they landed on the island.

Hamish looked at The Explorer.

The hands were pointing north-east.

But the watch wasn't glowing green any more.

It was like even The Explorer was wary of what was to come.

As the wind rose, the fog around them moved away for a second and Hamish caught sight of something and pointed.

'I think it's a sign,' he said.

'A sign?' said Alice, looking around. 'Of what?'

'No,' said Hamish, and he smiled. 'I think it's an actual sign . . .'

18

I Saw the Sign

Hamish felt a little weak at the knees.

This was a big deal.

If there was one thing he knew about a KEEP OUT sign, it was that it meant that somewhere behind it there must be something worth seeing.

And if one said:

NOTHING TO SEE HERE ... well, that just went double.

'That's what we head for,' said Hamish. 'The place where there's nothing to see.'

'Sounds like Starkley,' joked Alice.

The further they walked over craggy rocks, keeping low as they reached the brow of any hill, the louder and more intimidating a strange noise became.

It was like a **VOOOOOOOV**.

It just kept happening.

VOOOOV VOOOOV VOOOOOV.

The sort of noise you might imagine a wind farm makes, or a giant windmill. Regular, steady, loud and with the kind of power behind it that made your fringe flip and every hair on your arm stand to attention.

What if that was the noise of a Superior?

'Where's it coming from?' asked Alice, as the noise grew louder.

'Yuk,' said Hamish. 'Look at this . . .'

It was a black cactus – a blacktus. The plants on this island were horrible, as if nature itself didn't want visitors. The blacktus was tall, thick, waxy, spiky and whatever the other Spice Girl was called. A whole minefield of awful, sharp blackti stood rigid behind it.

'We'll have to go around,' said Alice, taking charge and pulling Hamish by the hand.

'Wait,' said Hamish, as they reached another small hill. 'Alice, not so fast!'

He could smell something. A putrid, pungent smell. The sort of smell that hits the back of your head with a thump. And it was a worryingly familiar smell . . .

Hamish clambered up a small hill, and peeked over the top.

'Look!' he said, and Alice peeked over too.

What they saw was incredible.

A vast field of Venus spytraps.

Thousands of them. Tens of thousands of them. Snapping heads, razor-sharp teeth, lolloping, viney arms.

A world of spytraps, as far as the eye could see.

It had been scary enough when the seeds had fallen on Starkley. Hamish had thought they'd taken care of the invasion, that it was a one-off. But looking at the field below it was clear that Earth had already been invaded. The seeds that had been brought to **FRYKT** were being raised. Raised to be an army!

'Those spytraps seem different,' said Alice, frowning, and she was right.

Were they asleep? They were swaying gently as the mysterious **VOOOOV**s rang through the air. These traps seemed docile.

All that was about to change in a big way, as the smell that still hung in the air grew stronger and the kids held their noses.

A Terrible came into view.

The same kind of awful, bilious monsters Alice, Hamish and the rest of the **PDF** had come up against before.

Monstrous, mallevalunt, murderous henchmen!

The Terrible wiped its tusks and trudged onwards. It was dragging a huge chunk of some kind of meat behind it, the size of an elephant's leg. The Terrible whistled as it did so, and now all the spytraps were awake all right. The smell must have alerted them. They stood to attention, straining and SNAPPING and spiking at each other.

The Terrible had a thick whip at its side. It snarled at the spytraps, who were almost barking at it, eagerly, sniffing the meat smell in the air. Hamish and Alice sank lower, trying to remain unseen, as the Terrible felt for its whip and cracked it at the traps, keeping them in line. Then it flung the hunk of meat into the very middle of the field. The traps began to fight each other, **CLACK-CLACK-CLACKING** away, each one desperate to be fed.

'They're so hungry,' whispered Alice, as Hamish watched the Terrible turn around and walk away. 'That one bit of food isn't enough for all of them!'

'The Superiors are keeping them hungry,' he said. 'Think about how moody you get when you haven't eaten in a while. You snap at people, don't you? That's what they want. They're starving the traps to keep them mean.'

Alice shook her head. 'It's cruel,' she said, sadly. 'It's like

when people mistreat dogs. They're treating them badly and making them worse.'

As the traps fought for the scraps of meat, Hamish scanned the horizon.

More black cacti. More sharp and craggy rocks. But over there, just beyond the field, what was that he could make out in the mist?

'The rope,' he said. 'The rope that goes up into nothing!'

Hamish and Alice knew they had to be very, very careful.

They'd been brave, stepping onto the island when all they'd

promised themselves they'd do would be to take a look from afar.

And now here they were, right in the middle of an enemy base – surrounded by spytraps and Terribles and who knew what else? One wrong move and they'd be toast!

But they had to get a closer look at that rope. What was it? Why did it go straight up in the air? Where did it lead? The **Holonow** had to have shown it to them for a reason, and it was surely key to finding out whatever the Superiors were up to.

They kept low and moved fast, darting between rocks and

jumping over sharp and toothy gaps, or strange, fizzing rock pools. They got closer, until Hamish could look up and see the very fibres of the huge rope on the other side of a hill.

'Up here,' he said, and pulled Alice alongside him, to where they could hide behind two steaming rocks.

Below, Terribles were everywhere. Dozens of them. Slanking around, festering about, gorging on meat, drinking bottles of blilk and laughing horribly.

Another hulked out from a low building, slapping its friends on the back with a wet palm and whispering something urgently.

Now the atmosphere changed.

If anything, you could call it an atmos-fear.

Something was coming. Something so horrible that even the Terribles were scared of it. They tossed away their blilk and stood to attention, only slightly quaking.

Hamish and Alice held their breath.

Superior Alert!

So this was a Superior.

Enemy of Earth!

Destroyer of Civilisations!

I would love to tell you that it had a wonderful, kind face.

Oh, I would love to tell you that it was tiny, with the lovely smooth fur of a dormouse and a little baseball cap that said **'Trees are ace!'**.

I would love to tell you it was kind to animals, and looked like an adorable kitten when it smiled, and was holding a direct-debit mandate for a regular standing order to several local charities.

BUT I CANNOT.

The first thing you noticed about a Superior was its body.

Tall.

Lean.

Muscular.

Like a . . . what? An upright dinosaur maybe?

Only then did you notice its head.

The head of a Venus spytrap!

But, instead of being green, its skin was darkest purple, with scales that seemed almost to have lives of their own. They cracked like leather and, on top of it all, the Superior wore a dirty white lab coat, like a slithery reptilian science teacher.

Its long, thick tail thrashed from side to side and reminded Hamish of a flexible tree trunk, swatting anything in its way to one side. Roots grew from the tip of the tail, scraping at the ground as if they were trying to find somewhere to grow.

Urgh!

As soon as it appeared, the Terribles fell to their fat knees, respectful of their master. They bowed their heads as two more giant Superiors stomped out of the building, growling and making sure no one was making eye contact.

More Terribles thundered towards the rope now, slowing to kneel in the shadow of whatever lay above. This was a sea of Terribles, and Hamish and Alice trembled as they cowered on the brow of the hill.

'TERRIBLES!' roared the first Superior. **'THE TIME IS CLOSE!'**

The Terribles rose to their feet and cheered.

'OUR EXPERIMENTS WITH THE HUMANS OF STARKLEY HAVE SHOWN US THE WAY.'

The Terribles cheered again, as the second Superior stepped forward.

'Before there was the Before,' it said. 'A time when anything seemed possible for us. Only in the Now did the humans begin to fight. Then there will be the Then! And that means an Earth ruled by us!'

A mighty cheer was followed by the thunder of hundreds of Terribles stamping their feet. Hamish and Alice swapped a fearful glance. They were so outnumbered. They inched closer to one another as the very ground beneath them shook.

'What do you think their plan is?' said Alice, over the din. 'What have they got up their sleeves?'

The **VOOOOOOOOV VOOOOOOOOV VOOOOOOOOV** of the invisible wind farm continued.

One of the Superiors stalked over to the giant rope in the centre of the circle, its splayed lizard feet scratching white scars in the concrete.

'BEHOLD!' it roared.

With one long finger, it pressed a button on a console at the foot of the rope.

Directly above, the clouds began to clear. The mists parted. The sky brightened.

Alice and Hamish strained their necks to see what could possibly be above them.

The noise of the **VOOOOOV**s soared, now, as right up there, right above them, lit by a shaft of golden sunlight, they saw an unbelievable sight.

'An AIRSHIP!' said Hamish, in awe.

It reminded him of the opening scene of Star Wars, one of his favourite films to watch with his dad. A massive battleship was revealed moment by moment in the movie and this was what he was seeing now as the clouds continued to part. As the air cleared, he could see it was long and yellowy-white, with eight ginormous turbines **VOOOOOV**ing slowly in the air. There was some kind of gun blaster at the front. It was the most enormous thing Hamish had ever seen.

The rope that kept the ship tethered to the ground was leaking water. It spurted and trickled and ran. And, now that they were closer, Hamish could see that it wasn't really a rope at all, but some kind of pipe. Hamish had read about nuclear power, in one of his long lunchtimes in the school library, before strange things had started happening all around him all the time. He remembered that water was needed to cool a nuclear reactor down. This water must be being pumped from the very heart of **FRYKT** and travelling up to the airship.

'**OUR SHOW OF STRENGTH AGAINST STARKLEY HAS PANICKED BELASKO. THEY HAVE MOVED THE NUCLEAR BALL FROM ITS PROTECTIVE BASE. BUT THEY ARE FOOLS! NOW IT IS OUT IN THE OPEN IT WILL BE FAR EASIER TO STEAL AND, WITH IT, OUR SHIP WILL BE CAPABLE OF CREATING THE GREATEST GRAVITATIONAL ANOMALY OF ALL TIME!**' roared the Superior.

Hamish and Alice looked at each other in alarm. The Superior was talking about a GravityBelch!

Hamish's head was spinning. When the GravityBurps were happening, Belasko had thought it was doing the right thing by moving the Nuclear Ball. In fact, it was doing exactly what the Superiors wanted!

'THE HUMANS WILL RISE UNTIL THEY CAN RISE NO MORE!' roared the Superior. **'THEY WILL BE SUCKED FROM THE PLANET IN THE BLINK OF AN EYE. ALL THAT WILL REMAIN WILL BE WHAT WE NEED TO MAKE THE PLANET OUR OWN! A WORLD IN WHICH WE GROW OUR OWN FOOD AND DINE LIKE ROYALTY!'**

One of the Superiors walked slowly to the edge of the spytrap field.

The traps around it seemed scared, and struggled and fought to get away. But they were rooted to the ground.

The Superior grabbed one of the traps, and yanked it from the soil, as the ones around it squealed and mewed.

The Superior **WOLFED** the spytrap down in one and wiped its mouth.

'They eat traps!' said Alice. 'We thought they were planting them on Earth to get us. In fact, they were doing some farming!'

'They want to make Earth a planet to grow their food!' said Hamish. 'And we have to stop them!'

But how? They had no idea where the Nuclear Ball was

and, if the Superiors managed to find out first and grab it, it would be curtains!

'ONE MORE TEST ON STARKLEY!' roared the first Superior, signalling to a Terrible, who brought out a walkie-talkie and barked something into it.

Around them, the winds grew stronger as the **VOOOOOOV**s became quicker. The turbines sped up and whipped around. Damp black leaves flew into the air, slapping into their faces. The moss on the ground began to rise like dust. Everyone stared up at the airship.

BOOOOOOM.

UUUUURRRRRRRRPPPPP.

An invisible ray seemed to tear up the sky and headed in the direction of Starkley. The gun at the head of the ship vibrated and rattled from the force of its shot.

'I hope everyone's inside!' said Alice, as the **UUUURRRRRPPPP** zinged away.

'We need to stop them before they get to a Belch,' said Hamish, but it seemed absolutely impossible. Here they were, just two kids, with no tech, no gadgets and no ideas. Stuck on an enemy island, far from home, with hundreds of Terribles, spytraps and Superiors. What could they possibly do?

'Hamish, we need to get out of here,' said Alice. 'Now we know how they're doing the Burps. It's the airship. If they've got the Nuclear Ball, then the next time they try it, it's going to be so much worse. We've got to go home and call the Air Force!'

Hamish knew Alice was right. They had to warn everyone.

And then he locked eyes with a sniffling, snortling **TERRIBLE**.

Escape from
FRYKT Island

'RUUUUUUUUN!' yelled Hamish, jumping from the brow of the hill and into a rock pool below.

But he didn't need to tell Alice. She was already down on the ground and six paces ahead of him.

The Terrible had spotted Hamish, but had been slow to react. It **HOWLED**, but its voice was lost in the noise of thunderous cheering coming from the other Terribles down below.

The kids had a head start and raced away with their hearts in their mouths, leaping over gaps and darting through the blackti, all the while aware that any second the chase might begin.

'Can you see the tug yet?' shouted Hamish, scanning the choppy coast, as Alice – still Starkley Under-12s 100-metre champion – kept her elbows high and her eyes on the ground. They couldn't afford even one stumble now.

'**THERE!**' came a mighty roar from the brow of the hill they'd just left.

The Terrible had finally managed to alert the others and a Superior pointed a clawed finger at Hamish and Alice, as they moved swiftly across the enemy island.

Six Terribles shot down the hill after the two children, their nails scraping and sparking off the rocks. They ran like dogs, all four feet slapping the ground and a trail of slather left in their wake.

But Hamish and Alice were fast. Down a second blackened hill they slid, finding their feet immediately and continuing their run.

A moment later, the Terribles slid too, but their feet gave way, sending them tumbling to the bottom in a mass of tusks and sweat.

'The mo-skis!' yelled Alice, pointing at the machines that were just where they'd left them. 'Get them to the water! Remember, Terribles hate water!'

They pushed their skis onto the ice, which cracked and splintered with more intensity than before, then jumped on.

Alice started hers and began to rev.

But Hamish's wouldn't start!

'Come on!' yelled Alice, turning back to look. The Terribles were on their feet now, and gaining fast, pounding towards them. 'Quickly, Hamish!'

But no matter what he did, it wouldn't start. It must have been waterlogged from all that spinning around!

'Get on mine!' shouted Alice.

Hamish jumped off his bike, the ice groaning and splintering beneath his feet as he landed. It was going to give way. He'd fall in and end up stuck in the freezing water!

Alice revved her engine as the six ghastly, slimery Terribles reached the ice, then stretched to grab Hamish with one hand as **_VOOOOOM!_**

The mo-ski lurched forward, sliding wildly on the ice and dragging Hamish behind it in a figure of eight.

He threw one leg over the seat and slapped Alice's back and shouted, 'GO!' just as the Terribles skittered and scattered on the ice behind him.

The ice finally gave way under their combined weight and CRACK-ASSSH! – the Terribles plunged deep into the water, clawing at the surface, trying to grab onto the back of the mo-ski.

Alice ROARED off, leaping from a wave like a ramp as the panicking Terribles paddled desperately for shore.

As soon as Hamish and Alice arrived back on the tug, Buster started the engine and pulled away. He pulled away at full throttle, but it was still far too slowly for everyone's liking.

The shoreline was by now packed with Terribles, each of them hungrily snarling at the boat as it disappeared. A black cloud of steam rose from their nasty, scaly bodies.

Alice had gone very quiet. She was always brave, but today she had seen just how powerful the enemy was. Once the Superiors got their hands on the **NUCLEAR BALL** – and Alice knew they would stop at nothing to get it – the world was doomed.

And what could a bunch of kids do about it?

Nothing.

'At least they don't know for sure it was us,' said Elliot, peering through his binoculars and then immediately deciding not to do that any more.

Buster stared at the Terribles. They were carrying Hamish's mo-ski back to their masters as some kind of trophy.

'I wouldn't be so certain,' he said. 'Each of the mopeds has "Slackjaw's Motors" written on the licence plate. It won't take them long to recognise them from the first time we foiled their plans.'

Alice shook her head, sadly. 'I would say Starkley's problems are just beginning,' she said.

'Why?' asked Venk, relieved to be moving at pace now.

'Because,' said Hamish, 'now they know we know.'

No one had noticed that Clover had gone completely and utterly white.

'Well, we just have to make sure they don't get the Nuclear Ball,' suggested Venk. 'Hamish, can you get a message to your dad? We need Belasko's help.'

That was all Hamish could think about too.

Clover was shaking now.

'Uh, guys . . .' she said, uncertainly.

'Good idea, Venk,' said Alice. 'We need to tell Belasko everything we know.'

'Um . . . guys?' said Clover again. 'GUYS!'

She was pointing at something in the sea. Her hand was trembling. Her lip was quivering.

Against all their instincts, the **PDF** turned to see the huge green stalk of the sea spytrap, bigger and greener and ghastlier than ever.

And it was shaking.

Waves crashed around it as it vibrated and hummed.

Seagulls took flight.

This thing was ready to pop!

'Get in the cabin!' yelled Hamish, as—

BOOOOOOOOOM!

Giant slivers of plant twisted and twirled through the air. They were the size of buses and SPLA-KASHED! as they landed in the sea.

Water flew everywhere. Gunk tumbled towards them.

Still the hulking plant RUMBLED and SHOOK as POP!

BLAAAAAFFF!

Its massive head appeared, rising out of the stalk, two ginormous eyes blinking in the sun as it was born.

CLACK!

CLACK!

CLACK!

Each of its teeth was MEGA!

Buster reached for the steering wheel, but there was no need.

The spytrap had risen with such force that it created ginormous waves as it stretched high into the sky. The waves now carried the tugboat away at a hundred miles an hour as the trap **CLACK-CLACK-CLACKED** at the clouds.

'**Whoooooooaaaa!**' yelled Elliot, holding onto his glasses with one hand and the boat with another.

On the boat sped towards Starkley, riding the foaming crest of a giant wave, with the PDF all thinking that the second they got home, there would be serious work to do.

Opposites
Attacked

The tug hit the beach with great force, carving up the sand like a hot knife through fudge.

'Hamish!' came a voice from the shore. 'What did you do? Where did you go?'

It was his dad! He was standing by his car with two Belasko agents, talking on radios and staring at the fiery explosion in the sea. They'd headed back to Starkley the very second the green sea plant had been reported.

'A spytrap, Dad!' said Hamish. 'A massive one in the sea!'

'Don't worry, we're on it,' his dad said. 'Please tell me you didn't go to **FRYKT**!'

'Of course we did,' said Alice, standing her ground. 'We saw the message on the Holonow. You told us to go and check the place out.'

'No,' said Hamish's dad. 'I was telling you to be careful and stay put. I was trying to tell you there was great danger!'

'Well, next time move to where you can get better reception,' said Alice, removing a starfish that had somehow got caught up in her hair as they sped to shore. 'Your voice was cutting out like crazy!'

'Hamish, that was really silly,' said his dad, taking him to one side.

Hamish had not been expecting that. His cheeks burnt red. Silly? It wasn't silly! It was brave and heroic and he was only trying to do the right thing!

'But the Nuclear Ball . . .' said Hamish.

'It's safe, pal. We moved it. We know what we're doing.'

'It's not safe!' said Alice, joining them, because now was not the time to let herself be left out. 'The Superiors wanted Belasko to move it,' she said, almost annoyed at him. 'It was part of their plan because they couldn't get to it. They made you panic, and now it's on its way somewhere, and it'll be far easier for them to snatch.'

'Then they're going to put it in their airship!' said Hamish.

'Airship?' said his dad.

'They've kept everyone away from **FRYKT** by controlling the weather somehow. And they hid an airship in the clouds, just like they probably hide stuff on Venus.'

Hamish was talking quickly now and his dad was struggling to keep up.

'And they've got water to cool the Nuclear Ball, so then they can use its power to do a GravityBelch and suck everyone off the planet! Then they're going to fill the place with spytraps and Earth will be theirs!'

Hamish's dad's expression changed from one of bravery to one of real worry. He moved away, got his radio out and barked into it.

'Status update on the package, please. Immediately.'

In all the excitement, the **PDF** had completely forgotten that Starkley had fallen foul of yet another GravityBurp.

As they arrived back in town in the ice-cream van, there were still people caught up in the big net above the town square. Others, in boots filled with rocks, were trying to fish them out with long hooks.

'That was a big one, eh?' yelled Mr Neate, from the top of a chimney.

Tree branches were pointing vertically. Cars were overturned. Hamish's friend Robin had lost yet another football. It looked like the end of the world.

Plus, it had completely knackered Madame Cous Cous's

International World of Treats. What a state it was in!

'Actually, that wasn't the Burp,' said Madame Cous Cous, looking furious as Hamish arrived. 'That was your little pet, "Vinnie".'

Hearing his name, Vinnie burst out of a display cabinet. He had nineteen lollipop sticks poking out of his mouth and a blissful look on his face.

Seeing his friend and master, the trap licked Hamish's face with such force that he was lifted off the ground. Vinnie's tongue was like sandpaper and he panted, eagerly, and licked Alice too.

'Yeuch, geroff, plant!' she yelled. 'Your tongue stinks of Cola cubes!'

Vinnie had lain waste to the sweet shop. Not one drawer remained closed; not one sweet remained unslathered-on. To apologise to Alice for his lick, Vinnie burped up a Twix from his tummy and spat it at her.

Madame Cous Cous looked exhausted.

'It's been through every sweet in the place!' she said. 'It's also eaten all my cereal, six plates of bacon and eggs, two chairs and a rug I bought to celebrate the Queen's coronation.'

Hamish smiled as Vinnie licked him again. It felt good to smile after everything that had happened.

'All it wants now is great big cones full of candyfloss!' said Madame Cous Cous, offering Vinnie another one.

'Just keep him away from those horrible Norwegian purple things,' said Alice. 'Crikey, can you imagine how many Candgrenades we'd need to tackle that massive one in the sea?' She laughed, even though this was no laughing matter, and Hamish glanced at her.

Through the window, Hamish saw his dad and the other **Belasko** agents walking towards the sweet shop, each of them holding a map and talking animatedly. He wished he was doing that too.

'Right,' said Dad, walking in. 'Oh—!' He saw Vinnie and jumped.

'This one's fine, Dad,' said Hamish, standing in front of his friend, protectively. 'He just likes sweets is all.'

'These Superiors you saw on **FRYKT**,' said Dad, ignoring this. 'How many of them were there?'

'Three Superiors,' replied Alice. 'Hundreds of Terribles. Thousands of spytraps. And who knows what was under the surface.'

Hamish's dad tapped his chin. 'We're going to order a complete evacuation of Starkley,' he said. 'It's time to cut our losses and move on.'

'Give up Starkley?' said Alice, shocked. 'Why? It's our home!'

'We'll find another one,' said Dad.

Hamish and Alice stared at each other, unable to believe what they were hearing. Leave Starkley? Sure, it may have had a reputation for being a bit boring, but that didn't mean the kids could just turn their backs on it. 'It's the only course of action, Hamish, and your mum'll be delighted,' his dad continued. 'Goonhilda Swag is making her life a misery. And, to be honest, Goonhilda is right: this isn't a proper town . . .'

Not a proper town? This was crazy. Where did grown-ups get their ideas? And they couldn't split up. Hamish and Alice – and their friends outside – were the **PDF**. And, more than that, they were best friends! Hamish understood that his dad was trying to keep them safe, but surely there had to be another way?

Hamish put a hand on his dad's strong arm. It felt a bit hot and trembly and Hamish noticed he almost seemed a bit panicky now. You always think grown-ups have a plan, but sometimes they're just making it up as they go along.

'It's okay, Dad,' said Hamish. 'I gave up too. But Alice made me see that there's always another way.'

His dad looked at him. 'And what is it?' he said. 'What's the other way?'

Hamish gulped. This was his chance to prove himself. But he'd said all that before he'd even had a chance of thinking what that other way might be. Now he was going to have to make it up as he went along!

'Um . . . it's . . . you know, we could . . .'

His dad nodded him on, giving him a chance to finish, keen to hear this great plan.

'Well, Hamish?' he said. 'What is it?'

In the distance, they could hear the intimidating wail of a siren. Was that Belasko? Or the Superiors? Whatever it was, a siren is rarely a good thing.

'Well, my idea,' said Hamish, struggling to come up with something, 'is . . . the opposite of yours.'

The words hung in the air.

'I'm sorry, Hamish. We have to go – we have to hide the Nuclear Ball,' said his dad. 'We need to act now.'

'What about this button everyone keeps mentioning?' said Alice out of desperation. 'What happens if we press it? Some kind of explosion?'

Hamish's dad shook his head.

'No. No buttons. Look, you did well to warn us what they

were planning. But now we must hide the ball and hope for the best.'

'Or,' said Hamish. 'The opposite.'

What kind of plan was that?

What was he suggesting? Not hide it and hope for the worst?

His dad once told him it was good to challenge things. To find options where there don't seem to be any. His dad said that was thinking outside the box.

'How do you mean the opposite?' said Dad.

'We . . . give them the Nuclear Ball?' said Hamish.

The other Belasko agents sighed. But Hamish's dad nodded him on, encouragingly.

'We want the Superiors to go away without the Nuclear Ball, right?' said Hamish, and suddenly a plan somewhere far behind his eyes clicked into place. 'Well, how about instead we try and get them to come here, and then we give them what they want?'

Hmmm. Er. Well.

Dad's plan to evacuate Starkley was in full force. Belasko agents drove from house to house. Long removal lorries started to arrive in town. The streetlights flashed red and blue.

As soon as Hamish had said they should give the Superiors exactly what they wanted, everyone had quickly stopped listening – it was clearly too much for a ten-year-old boy to handle and they reckoned he'd finally lost it. You'd think he'd have felt small and silly. But Hamish knew he was onto something. Somewhere deep inside he was sure he had the beginnings of a crazy idea.

He pulled Alice back inside the sweet shop.

'I don't get it,' she said. 'Why did you say that? Why did you say we should bring the Superiors closer to Starkley?'

'So we can give them the Nuclear Ball,' said Hamish, still not making much sense.

'We don't have the Nuclear Ball!' said Alice. 'And, even if we did, isn't the whole point that we don't want them to have it!'

'Not that Nuclear Ball,' he said. 'Our own Nuclear Ball.'

22

What's the Plan, Hamish?

'**It could work**,' said Elliot, striding around his war room. 'It just seems incredibly unlikely to.'

'But there's still a chance?' Hamish asked.

'Well, there's a chance I might turn into a lopsided French baguette called Nigel in the next five minutes,' said Elliot. 'But that doesn't mean I will.'

Once Hamish had told Alice his plan, they'd run straight to the first person he needed for his plan to work. But Madame Cous Cous hadn't been easy to convince.

'It goes against everything I wish to do!' she'd said, waving her stick around and handing Vinnie another massive candyfloss cone. 'They are the last people I want to talk to!'

Nevertheless, as Hamish and Alice had begged so nicely, and because this might be their last-ever days in Starkley, she'd agreed to make the calls he'd asked her to, and promised to try her best to make it happen.

With Madame Cous Cous on board, Hamish had gathered the **PDF** together in Elliot's war room and now that he had some backup, and a clear plan, it was time to talk to his dad again.

'This is our town, Dad,' Hamish said, pleading, as Agent Angus Ellerby strode around the town square, supervising the evacuation. 'We need to fight for it. Okay, so it's a bit of a boring place. But it's our boring place. I was born here. We were all born here.'

'I wasn't,' said Buster. 'I was born in Frinkley.'

Hamish shot him a look that said: You're not helping.

'The point is,' said Alice, reaching for Mister Ellerby's sleeve, 'everything we know comes from Starkley. This town is us. Would the **PDF** ever have happened without a town like Starkley? Would we ever have met?'

Hamish's dad smiled, gently.

'Sometimes to win, kids, you need to know when you've lost.'

'Who's trying to win kids?' asked Venk, confused. 'Was there a competition?'

'Please, Dad,' said Hamish. 'I can't pretend I understand

everything that's going on. I don't understand why the Superiors keep targeting Starkley. But I know that we are strong, and that there must be a reason for all this!'

'Please just listen to Hamish's plan, Mr Ellerby,' said Alice.

'There's no time,' said Dad. 'I wanted to give you a chance, Hamish, honestly I did, but now it's time for the grown-ups to take charge.'

'But you just want to give up. Is that what being a grown-up means, Dad? Giving up?'

Hamish watched his dad consider his words. This felt so unfair. It was like the more Hamish proved himself, the more he needed to keep proving himself.

So Hamish kept talking. He told his dad he knew his plan was a risk, that he knew it might not come off, but that if they all worked together, and just believed in it, then it might just succeed.

He talked clearly and with real passion in his eyes, while Alice stood right by his side, her eyes shining with pride in her best friend.

And, when he had stopped listening, Hamish's father put his hands behind his back, thought deeply and very carefully, and took out his radio.

'Stop the evacuation,' he said. 'New plan.'

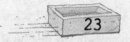

23

Secrets and Spies

On paper, you really could argue that not much had changed about Hamish's plan.

In fact, seeing as all this is already on paper, let's look at Hamish's new list.

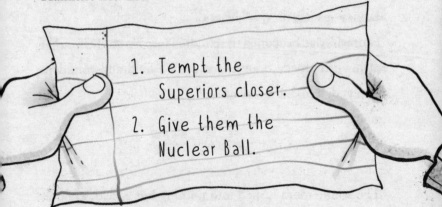

1. Tempt the Superiors closer.

2. Give them the Nuclear Ball.

You might think this seems like a terrible plan. But, as with all the best ideas, it was all in the detail.

'If this doesn't work, pal,' said Dad, who remained to be convinced, but like his son was willing to believe, 'that's the end of everything. The end of Starkley. The end of Belasko. Maybe even the end of the world.'

That was quite a lot of pressure to put on a ten-year-old's shoulders. Hamish almost wilted.

'It will work,' said Alice, sternly. 'Because we're the **PDF**.'

'So we need to get the Superiors' airship to fly closer to Starkley,' said Dad.

'How are we going to get them to do that?' asked Buster, concerned. 'We're Britain's fourth most boring town. No one wants to take a closer look.'

Dad smiled. That was it. 'So you want to know what makes Starkley special, do you?' he said.

Hamish's dad beckoned the children into his study, brought out his little metal orange, and with a loud and confident voice said, 'Holonow – play!'

FLASH!

The whole room turned into nothing but a field, as far as the eye could see.

Somewhere a cow mooed. Elliot moved his feet and heard them squelch in the holo-mud.

And weirdly everything was black and white.

'I think the Holonow might be on the blink!' said Buster. 'Try hitting it.'

'No, look,' said Venk. 'We're still in colour.'

That was odd. Why was everything else in black and white?

'**STARKLEY!**' came a voice from behind, and Hamish steeled himself for whatever he was about to learn about Britain's fourth most boring town.

Vapidia Sheen strode between them in wellington boots, pointing importantly, as the numbers . . .

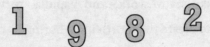

. . . zoomed through the room and hovered in front of her, before whooshing off again.

'In 1982, there was no Starkley,' said Vapidia. 'Just these fields and a cow with bronchitis.'

'MOO-chooo!' sneezed the cow.

'Oh, just what I was hoping for,' said Buster. 'A history lesson about fields and a cow with a cold.'

'No,' said Hamish, excited. 'This is more like time travel!'

'But these were no ordinary fields,' continued the hologram of Vapidia. 'These fields were special.'

In the distance, they could see a group
of men and women milling about. They were wearing
black boiler suits and holding clipboards. One of them was
pointing at the ground and smiling. Then they all shook
hands.

'Work on Starkley began immediately. Work that would
affect all humankind.'

Hamish stared closer at the group of people in the distance.
What was that on their boiler suits? Was that a Belasko
logo?

'Belasko set to work,' said Vapidia, 'with one aim in
mind: to create the fourth most boring town in Britain!'

Around them, all at once, bricks flew through the air,
landing on top of each other until they'd built boring, boxy
houses . . . it was like a sort of Lego advert. But real!

'They built houses! Shops! Schools!'

The kids ducked as more bricks flew through the air,
creating Winterbourne School.

'Everything you would expect from a modern, boring town!'

Thousands of bricks whooshed past, and now Starkley was
in colour, as the high street took shape around them.

Lord of the Fries!

The Tooth Hurts!

Pizza the Action!
British Hairways!

'But WAAAAAIT!' yelled Alice, so loudly that everyone jumped.

'Pause!' said Dad and, just like when you pause a video, everything stopped still around them.

'Why?' asked Alice, in the silence. 'Why would anyone want to build Britain's fourth most boring town? It makes no sense whatsoever! Why not build . . . Paris? Or Moscow?'

'Or Milton Keynes?' said Buster. 'They've got an ice rink in Milton Keynes. And you can go indoor skydiving.'

Dad smiled. 'Wait and you'll see. Play!' he said.

'Everything about Starkley was designed to blend in,' Vapidia continued. 'To avoid attention. To deter scrutiny. Starkley was scientifically engineered to be **DULL.**'

She walked around the town, pointing at things.

'Every sign – brown. The only landmark – an old grey bridge. The town slogan – **"NO OFFENCE IF YOU'VE SOMEWHERE ELSE TO BE!"** A town where the streetlights are a little dimmer. The restaurants close a little earlier. A town that holds no promise. A place that doesn't stand out.'

'Why would they design it to be fourth most boring?' said Buster. 'Why not go the whole way?'

'Because the most boring town would get attention,' said Hamish, who was starting to piece it all together. 'But who cares about the fourth most boring town?'

'Only in Britain's fourth most boring town could Belasko feel safe from its enemies,' said Vapidia.

'Okay, but wait,' pleaded Alice, losing patience. 'Why build a town at all, if you were just going to hide it?'

Dad stopped the hologram, immediately transforming the room back to how it had been before.

'Because, Alice, Starkley has a bigger secret,' he said, clapping his hands together. 'Something incredible. Something amazing. Something that might just be the key to your plan, Hamish!'

The kids all stared up at him as he took a deep breath and revealed what he'd been longing to tell them.

'Starkley . . . is the most important place on the planet.'

They all kept staring at him.

Buster scratched his chin. Clover frowned.

Hamish's dad had gone mad, hadn't he?

'Sorry, Mr Ellerby,' said Elliot, 'but, uh, is that a sort of "dad" joke?'

Hamish's dad shook his head.

'No,' he said. 'Starkley is the most important place on the planet.'

Still no one seemed to quite believe him.

'Starkley? Our Starkley?' frowned Clover.

'Yes. Our Starkley,' said Hamish's dad, who didn't seem to understand why they found this so hard to believe. It was so easy. Literally all he was telling them was that out of all the hundreds of thousands of towns, cities, villages, hamlets, rural retreats, parks, towns, regions, counties, islands, metropolises, megalopolises, Mrs Chopalopalises, nations, states, back gardens, front lawns, understair cupboards, secret dens and countries on the planet – it was their little town that mattered the most of all. Simple.

'But . . . but we don't even have a McDonald's in Starkley!' said Buster. 'Or a cinema! You can buy hot dogs in Frinkley! With all onions and stuff! Mum said they're getting a Laser Quest!'

'How can Starkley be more important than anywhere else?' demanded Alice, hands on her hips, like she wasn't to be messed with any further.

'Because has anywhere else,' said Dad, starting to smile, 'got a special, secret hidden button?'

The kids all went, 'Ooooh!'

Finally, Hamish was about to find out about the button!

Everybody loves a button.

Here's a picture of a button.

You want to press it, don't you?

Here's a picture of another button.

I've put DO NOT PRESS on it.

You still want to, though, don't you?

Now I've put a

TERRIFYING SKULL AND CROSSBONES on it too.

It's probably **POISONOUS!**

Yet now you want to press it more than ever! What is wrong with you?!

So imagine hearing that hidden somewhere near your home was a super-secret hidden button. One that had been there since the day the town was built. One you'd never ever heard about until recently. And, what's more, you have absolutely no idea what it does.

Now that's a button you'd want to press, isn't it?

'It's time!' said Dad into his phone, leading the kids towards the town clock. 'Code K.'

Immediately, all the streetlights in Starkley started flashing red and blue again, like the top of a police car or ambulance. A siren rang out, and the bells on Winterbourne School started to ring and, somewhere up above, blackbirds took flight.

Belasko agents poured from a coach that had been ready to squirrel people out of town, as Hamish's dad rallied the people of Starkley around the town clock.

Moments later, they were joined by some familiar faces.

Madame Cous Cous.

Mr Slackjaw.

Frau Fussbundler.

Mr Longblather.

What were they doing walking to the clock with such purpose? Why did they look so serious? So . . . important?

'Hello, team,' said Hamish's dad.

Hamish frowned. Team?

Each of them moved forward, gave Hamish a small smile and silently took out a key.

For Madame Cous Cous, it was the key to the sweet shop.

For Mr Slackjaw, the key to his biggest Vespa.

For Frau Fussbundler, it was the big brass key to Winterbourne School.

For Mr Longblather, the tiny silver one for Brenda, his rusty 1984 Vauxhall Nova in terrier brown.

'Every spy organisation has sleeper agents,' said Dad. 'In a town as boring as Starkley, we decided on sleepy agents. Four brave souls who have remained embedded in Starkley – only to be activated at a time of true and awesome peril.'

None of them looked sleepy now. They looked alive and alert. Each made a very serious face as they stepped up to the town clock. At last, this was their moment!

Hamish had never noticed before, but on each side of the clock tower, at about eye level, was a tiny hole.

The grown-ups slid their keys into these slits and turned.

A hidden flap at the front of the tower thumped down.

And inside . . . was a bright red button.

'It's time to reveal Starkley's biggest secret,' said Dad. 'Hamish . . . why don't you do the honours?'

Button It,
Hamish!

Hamish moved his finger closer to the button and then paused.

What would the button do?

Well, let's find out.

The very moment he pressed it down with a satisfying **THUCK**, the ground beneath his feet started to shake and judder.

The concrete on the streets began to move and crack.

The whole town began to vibrate.

What was this – an earthquake button?

'Oh my days!' yelled old Mr Neate, grabbing onto a bench as the balls of his feet skittered around on the ground so much he looked like he was tap-dancing.

The hands of the town clock began spinning round and round and round, as right across the town square whole buildings started slowly to move.

CRUUUUUUNCH.

'Hamish!' yelled a just-arrived Grenville, furious. 'Why are you demolishing our town? Stop it at once!'

But if you looked closely – really closely – you'd see that these buildings weren't being demolished.

In fact – they were getting stronger!

Winterbourne School was first to transform.

As its very foundations began to scream, the old building actually raised itself higher, like it was stretching after a long sleep, with a whole new level now bursting from the ground.

Soil and dust blew everywhere.

PFFFFFFF.

Grey metal grilles slid from the walls to cover every window.

SHUUUUUNK.

An enormous metal siren broke through the tiles on its roof, causing the school bell to fall to the ground with a dull thud.

The siren sang its song:

VWOOOOOOOOOWVVVV!

Now, across town, the whole of Slackjaw's Motors literally flipped itself over – WHOOOMPF – to reveal a brand-new, domed building that had been underneath all along. The old Slackjaw's Motors was now underground, and a new, computerised sign read **WEAPONS & TECH.**

'Weapons and tech? What the heck?' said Grenville.

'This is no time for poetry, Grenville,' said Alice. 'This is a time for wonder!'

Madame Cous Cous's International World of Treats was splitting in two now, its walls rumbling as they slid apart.

Inside, as brick dust filled the air, all the shelves and trays that had been holding sweeties and chocolates for all these years simply disappeared into the walls. Out slid shelves of microscopes, Petri dishes, sample pots and a huge sign saying **SCIENCE LABORATORY.**

Hamish looked at Madame Cous Cous while this was happening. She didn't seem at all surprised. She'd known all along this day might come. She'd been ready.

All over town, benches flipped over to reveal sleek telescopes that had been hidden in the ground beneath them. Phone booths turned into **COMMUNICATION CENTRES**, with little satellite dishes suddenly bursting through their ceilings and sniffing around in the air. Metal shutters slid across the windows of every house they could see. The bus stop turned itself into an airtight

AIR-RAID SHELTER.

And now, right next to them all, the town clock which had been doing nothing but shuddering, suddenly extended itself up out of the ground. A whirring metal pivot burst through the concrete and bent the clock at an angle.

BVVVVVVT!

It aimed itself towards **FRYKT** and the innocent town clock had become a massive, fearsome missile.

Starkley had transformed itself into what it had always been designed to be – what the Superiors had always suspected it to be – Earth's first line of defence against whatever threat may arise!

I told you: sometimes the most ordinary things can be the most special.

'So, for the first time,' said Hamish, 'Starkley is not hidden in plain sight!'

'Today,' said Dad, importantly, 'we want to be seen.'

And they had their wish.

In the distance, above **FRYKT**, the clouds began to clear.

VOOOOOOV VOOOOOOV VOOOOOOV s filled the air.

The Superiors were watching.

Let's Go!

Time was of the essence.

Now that the Superiors had seen Starkley reveal itself, they would absolutely want a closer look.

Well, of course they would. They would probably be congratulating themselves. The Superiors had been creating GravityBurps to panic Belasko so they would move the Nuclear Ball. But the secret organisation were obviously so terrified that they'd revealed their hidden base too. And it was the small town of Starkley. A place the Superiors had always suspected was at the centre of something.

If Starkley was so wonderfully defended . . . then it stood to reason that it must be defending something wonderful.

The Superiors would not have had to think too carefully before deciding that Starkley was obviously hiding the **NUCLEAR BALL**.

Now the Superiors had the chance not just to grab the

power they needed, but to destroy their enemy's base at the same time.

Oh, this would be easy, they must have been thinking.

The **PDF** knew they had to take advantage of this intergalactic arrogance.

For the rest of the day, Belasko set about securing the town, setting up agents in every house they could. There was an agent at every telescope, and one in every communications centre, and Hamish's dad moved from person to person, making sure they knew what Hamish's plan was.

'We're going to give them exactly what they want!' he barked. 'Nobody do anything until they've got the ball!'

With the **PDF** all fully briefed, Hamish sat down for his dinner.

'An army marches on its stomach!' Hamish's grandma had used to say, which had always confused Jimmy, who'd thought armies definitely marched on their feet.

Hamish's dad had said that the plan was too dangerous for the **PDF** to handle alone so the Belasko agents would be in charge. Because it was their idea, the **PDF** were being allowed to help at the start, so long as they then did what they were told.

Hamish was pleased that the **PDF** was going to be part of the plan he'd come up with. But he couldn't help but be slightly cross that his dad and the other agents were still pushing them all aside.

The grown-ups might not be confident in his friends but Hamish was sure the **PDF** knew what they were doing. Elliot reckoned the Superiors would want maximum daylight, so would arrive at daybreak. Clover had found official Belasko boiler suits. Buster was bringing two-way radios. They'd arranged to meet up after dinner and set to work.

As Dad doled out chips and beans and more chips, Jimmy sat down. He was wearing headphones and listening to recordings he'd made of his own bad poetry. He said he was thinking of changing his name to **'DJ JIMMY LYRICIS'** and needed forty pounds to release an album called Jimmy Jimmy RhymeTime. He didn't seem quite as worried about the potential end of the world as other people were.

Hamish's mum was equally preoccupied.

'Oh, things just get worse and worse!' She sighed holding up a print-out of an email.

PUBLIC OFFICE OF PRIDE

From the desk of Goonhilda Swag

ADVANCE NOTICE OF THE SURPRISE VISIT

Dear Mrs Ellerby,

This is just a polite advance warning of the totally surprise visit that POP (not POOP) will be making in order to ascertain just how much of a mess your 'town' is.

Please ignore the fact that I have warned you about this surprise visit and carry on as normal. Probably best if you pretend it isn't happening. But it is. Though I haven't told you that. I'm just dying for you to know.

See you very soon,

Goonhilda Swag

'I don't get it,' said Mum. 'So is there a surprise visit or isn't there?'

'Don't you worry, my love,' said Hamish's dad. 'It'll all work out in the end.'

Hamish looked at his dad. Why had he said that? Because what if it didn't all work out in the end? With Goonhilda and the Superiors? Maybe his dad was just saying that to make them all feel better and part of Hamish liked this because it did make him feel safer. But it also made him feel like even after everything, including Hamish's upcoming plan, his dad wasn't being totally open. Things were about to get dangerous. Surely they had to be honest with each other?

But then Hamish knew he wasn't being honest either. He was upset his dad still wasn't taking the **PDF** seriously. Hamish wasn't sure he even wanted to tell the truth. What if his dad was annoyed at him? What if he went off again?

Or what if he thought Hamish was getting ideas above his station and stopped listening to his ideas?

So Hamish just ate his chips and kept quiet.

ЖЖ

It was nearly eight o'clock at night and the sky was beginning to darken.

Hamish was relieved. Darkness meant security.

He led his friends to Madame Cous Cous's International World of Treats, which since he'd pressed the button was now, of course, the **STARKLEY INTERNATIONAL SCIENCE LABORATORY**.

If all was going according to plan, then in just a few minutes' time the lab would be expecting visitors.

Visitors that Madame Cous Cous would not be thrilled to receive.

As you know, Hamish had revealed his plan to her that morning. He'd done it by saying, 'I have a special mission for you. We need your contacts!'

'My contacts!' she had replied. 'Of course. Hang on – I wear glasses, not contacts.'

'Your contacts in the sweet world,' Hamish had clarified, with no time for incredibly bad jokes.

Madame Cous Cous had stared at him, blankly.

'How on earth are they going to help?' she'd said. 'What – are you short on Chomps?'

'The people we seek are dangerous. We need those who are capable of creating something of true devastation!' Hamish had said.

Alice had stepped forward, importantly.

'Madame Cous Cous,' she'd said. 'We need NORWEGIANS.'

Madame Cous Cous brought both hands to her mouth. Her eyeballs doubled in size.

'No!' she said, a moment later. 'Not . . . **Norwegians!**'

And now, as Hamish waited nervously in the shop, the low growl of an approaching vehicle filled the room.

Outside, a red, white and blue motorcycle and sidecar pulled up.

They had arrived.

Into the shop walked two unusual men.

One very tall, bald man in a top hat with a twirly moustache.

And another, much shorter and wearing a beret and a monocle.

'Hei!' said the tall one.

'Hallo!' said the short one.

Madame Cous Cous's face darkened.

'Erik and Viktor Viktorius!' she seethed. 'You rotten Viking grotbags!'

Told you she wouldn't be pleased to see them.

'How lovely to see you again, Madame Cous Cous,' said Viktor, politely bowing, but Madame Cous Cous did not seem impressed.

'Do you know exactly how long I have been trying to sell your Goat Cheese Gobstøppers?' she barked.

Erik looked sheepish and twirled his thick blond moustache.

'They are an acquired taste?' he explained, smiling uncomfortably.

'A taste that has gone un-acquired for years!' spat Madame Cous Cous. 'And that's to say nothing of your Salted Fish Bålls. Or your Oslo Østrich Gum! I tried one of your

Såndefjord Sandals last year!'

'What's a Såndefjord Sandal?' asked Hamish.

'Disgusting!' said Madame Cous Cous. 'All leathery. Took me a week to eat one!'

'Those aren't actually sweets,' said Erik. 'They're literally just sandals.'

'We received your message and came swiftly,' said Viktor, trying to move things on. 'How can we help you? Perhaps you might like to reorder some quality Norwegian candies?'

'**ReORDER** some?' yelled Madame Cous Cous. 'I haven't **SOLD** one yet! Actually, that's not entirely true. I sold one five years ago to a small child named Philately Burble. She immediately grew a beard. Her parents tried to sue.'

'You might want to take a seat, Mr and Mr Viktorius,' said Hamish. 'I'm afraid the fate of the world is at risk and you might be our only hope.'

'Please explain,' said Viktor, cracking a knuckle, not for one second realising he was in for the challenge of a lifetime.

Are You Crazy?

There was no time to lose!

Inside Starkley International Science Laboratory, the kids had set straight to work.

Erik and Viktor Viktorius had thrown themselves into the plan too: barking orders, looking up old recipes, and beginning to craft a marvellous concoction using all the Petri dishes and mixing bowls that Madame Cous Cous could find.

They tasted. They sniffed. They seasoned. They shook their heads and started again.

'More Tabasco! More soy!' yelled Viktor Viktorius. 'And bring us a compacting machine!'

Buster had his spanner out.

Clover sucked on liquorice and mixed paints.

Elliot did sums and measurements.

Venk made the tea.

Vinnie sat in the corner, munching on a candyfloss cone, every now and again trying to take a lick of whatever it was the Norwegians were making.

'Careful, pal!' Hamish had to say each time, before realising, slightly embarrassed, that he'd called Vinnie 'pal'.

The air was thick with sweet-dust – great colourful puffs of sugary mist rising from bowls dotted all around the lab and coating every finger-marked surface. Alice walked around with a small fan, wafting dust from people's faces and guiding it out of the window.

They worked through the evening. They worked through the night. They were hot and sweaty and focused in this dimly lit room and, as the clock ticked closer to five in the morning, they realised they were close.

'Okay!' said Hamish, as Mr and Mr Viktorius slumped heavily into armchairs, covered in sugar and shattered. 'Over to Clover!'

And half an hour later – when they'd woken Clover and set her to work – it was complete.

It looked amazing.

※

'Oh my word!' shrieked Frau Fussbundler, who'd been standing guard outside Lord of the Fries with her umbrella.

'Then it's true!'

'It is!' said Mr Longblather, amazed at what he was seeing.

They watched in awe as the sun began to rise over Starkley and the **PDF** proudly pushed the fruits of their labour down the street.

Five kids pushing what at first sight appeared to be an enormous yellow boulder.

They had created their own Nuclear Ball!

It was the size of a Mini Metro. Perfectly round. Bright yellow, with black hazard markings all over it, and the words:

NOTICE: THIS IS A NUCLEAR BALL

Clover had sucked on six liquorice sticks to perfect the paintwork. Buster had added fake rivets and metal panels. It looked just like the one they'd seen in the **Holonow**.

To all intents and purposes, it was the same.

Except for one crucial difference.

'Keep away from it!' yelled Grenville, alarmed, spotting it for the first time as it trundled heavily past the town clock. 'I saw a programme all about nuclear things. You give that a sniff and your ears fall off. Or your feet will grow extra feet and run away. You should be wearing washing-up gloves! That stuff is super dangerous!'

Hamish smiled at the others.

'That's just what we want the Superiors to think,' he said.

'Hang on,' said Grenville, wrinkling his nose up and studying the ball a little more closely. 'I recognise that smell . . .'

And indeed he did.

Because they had not spent the whole night creating a giant Nuclear Ball.

Are you crazy?

They'd spent the whole night creating a giant Scandi Candgrenade!

It was Alice who'd given Hamish the idea, the day before, when she'd looked at the sea monster and said: 'Can you imagine how many Candgrenades we'd need to tackle that?'

Well, imagine indeed. Now imagine what would happen if the Superiors sucked this enormous, explosive edible up into their airship. They'd put it straight in the water tanks, thinking it was a **NUCLEAR BALL** that needed cooling down.

What would happen to the billions of tiny pieces of industrial-strength Norwegian popping candy when they did that? Think about what happened to the spytraps! Think about what happened to Grenville's bottom!

The Superiors' airship would explode.

There'd be no more GravityBurps.

No GravityBelch.

And no threat to life on Earth!

It was a brilliant plan.

꿔

As the sun rose over the sea, it brought with it the distant sound of the airship.

VOOOOOOOV.
VOOOOOOOV.
VOOOOOOOV.

But was it getting louder? Closer?

'The ball looks great Hamish!' yelled Dad. 'Okay – Belasko! We need to make this look as real as possible!'

Immediately, two Belasko lorries appeared from the new super-high-tech doors of Slackjaw's Motors. Agents sat in the cabins, with the visors on their helmets pulled right down. Mr Slackjaw himself was in a Belasko uniform and saluted Hamish and the team as he watched the lorries leave.

'We need to make it look like we're moving the Nuclear Ball out of Starkley!' said Dad, who'd drawn up a map for everyone to study.

'The Superiors have already seen what's happened to the town. They think they've put so much pressure on us that we've had to reveal our secret base. They'll be taking a closer look soon to see where we've hidden the ball. We need them to think we're moving it and they've caught us off guard.'

'We're going to head for the tugboat,' said Hamish. 'They'll think we're trying to hide the ball at sea. That's when Belasko will take over and let them have it – in all senses of the phrase!'

VOOOOOOOV. VOOOOOOOV. VOOOOOOOV.

The noise was definitely getting louder. Elliot had been right. The Superiors had waited until daybreak.

And now they were on their way.

'To the coast!' yelled Hamish.

27

Have a Ball!

Did you know that only **3** per cent of plans ever work?

Did you also know that more than **42** per cent of statistics are entirely made up?

Either way, the chances of this plan working out felt like they were dropping by the minute.

For a start, Hamish knew that for it to really, truly work, the **NUCLEAR BALL** couldn't be hidden in a lorry. No, the Superiors had to be able to see it from the air.

But as he, Alice, Buster, Elliot and Clover pushed the ball through town, dressed in full Belasko uniforms – then down the rickety steps towards the rocky path to the coast – there was trouble they hadn't anticipated. Small pieces of their Nuclear Ball kept being chipped away.

'That's not good,' said Venk, who was following behind, pulling Vinnie in the old tartan shopping trolley. It felt right that Vinnie should be there to see the kids put an end to his evil masters.

Hamish looked at the ball. Little cracks appeared every time they hit another unexpected bump in the road.

'The ball is getting **dirtier!**' said Elliot, concerned, and trying to stay in control of it. 'And **muddier!**'

'It has to stay bright yellow!' said Clover, desperately trying to colour bits in from a small paint pot she'd put in her pocket for emergencies.

Hamish's dad had chosen a good route from town which allowed the Belasko lorries to follow on the road close behind, making the whole thing look like an official convoy. The more convincing it looked, the better, and right now it looked pretty convincing. The **PDF** would push the ball all the way to the tugboat, ready for the grown-ups to take over and sail the ball to sea. The Superiors would see the ball and steal it, then boom! Hamish and the **PDF** would be able to watch the fallout from the coast.

But then – disaster.

'Oops!' said Buster, tripping over his laces, and pushing the ball ahead of them by a few metres.

'It's okay!' said Hamish, as they raced to try and catch up with it, but it wasn't okay, because the ball was now always just out of reach.

229

'No!'

said Alice.

It was rolling away on its own!

They were losing control!

'Come on!' said Hamish. 'We need to keep it on the road!'

But, as the street sloped downwards towards the coast, the ball picked up speed.

'Grab it!' yelled Elliot.

But how do you grab a ball? There's nothing to hold on to! Especially when it's so convincingly heavy and so wonderfully smooth and now moving faster and faster...

'SCRAAAWWWWLL!' yelled Vinnie, bouncing in the trolley behind them, sensing that

this runaway
ball was not part
of the gang's plan.
 The fake Nuclear Ball bounced
from one side of the street to the other as it
gained speed, crashing into parked cars and clipping

wing mirrors right off. Bins clattered and flew, tossing rubbish everywhere. Cats fled. The ball picked up more dints and dents and thundered on down the hill. It was like the worst game of pinball ever.

Through a puddle it splashed, the kids hot on its heels. The water in the puddle fizzed and sparked from the tiny chipped pieces of Candgrenade left in its wake.

'It's going off-road!' screamed Alice, as the ball hit the kerb with a **BANG** and now began to **BOUNCE** through a field, heading at great speed towards the coastal path.

The lorries couldn't follow any further now.

'We'll meet you down by the tug!' shouted Hamish's dad from the first lorry as they followed the road. 'Don't do anything without us!'

'But Dad!' yelled Hamish.

'Don't do ANYTHING!'

Hamish turned as the kids pelted into the field to chase their only hope against the Superiors.

What did Dad mean, don't do anything? What if he had to do something?

The ball was getting muddier and muddier now, as it tore through the field and down towards the cliffs. Rabbits ran from bushes. Squirrels bounded up trees. Foxes and badgers scarpered from the thunderous din.

'If that ball goes over the cliff and into the sea, it's all over!' yelled Hamish. 'We have to stop it!'

'The fence!' yelled Alice, pointing at the old wooden fence at the end of the field. 'The fence will stop it!!'

CRASH!

The ball smashed through the fence like it hadn't even been there and continued to roll, not slowing for a second. This was a disaster!

'Wait! Look!' shouted Hamish, suddenly finding hope. 'Mud!'

The field at the edge of the cliff was wet and brown. But, even if the mud stopped the ball, all they'd have to show for their great plan was a chipped and muddy ball. Hamish's dad and Belasko were heading for the tugboat. This wasn't where they'd agreed to meet at all.

This plan was going wrong seriously quickly: **94** per cent of plans do. But . . .

'It's slowing down!' yelled Clover, pelting through the broken fence.

And it was.

The ball – which had looked unstoppable just moments

ago – was sinking into the mud, carving a dent into the ground behind it as it rolled.

But was that enough?

Just as it was nearing the very edge of the perilous cliff, over which it would be lost to the sea forever . . .

It cluuuuuuunkered to a stop.

'Oh thank goodness!' yelled Buster, huffing and puffing as the gang and Vinnie caught up with it. The ball was safe. Teetering on a cliff edge, but safe.

'Look at it!' said Clover, sadly.

It was filthy. Damaged.

It no longer looked anything like a Nuclear Ball.

It looked like a giant, manky Malteser.

'I'll repaint what I can!' said Clover, bringing out her tiny pot, but already knowing she'd brought nowhere near enough.

And as she tried her best to quickly slather yellow paint over mud, and did nothing but create a sort of beige mush, the wind rose.

Though this was no ordinary wind.

The kids were used to the sea breeze down here on the coast, but this was a stronger wind altogether. This was a menacing wind.

234

They'd been so busy screaming and running and chasing the ball that they'd not yet noticed what else was in the air.

The harsh hum of **VOOOOOVS**.

Hamish looked up as a looming shadow crept over his gang, blocking out the sky from view.

The Superiors were right above them.

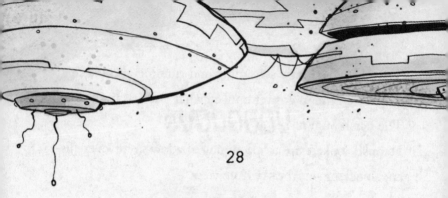

28

Superior Intellect

Hamish knew his dad had told him not to do anything. That meant run away or hide. Keep out of trouble and danger until the Belasko agents got there. But who knew when that would be.

Hamish Ellerby was a good boy, but enough was enough.

This was not a time to just do what he was told.

This was not a time to run, or hide.

This was a time to act.

Just like Alice had so confidently said in the great sweet shop spytrap siege – you don't need permission to save the world!

Hamish burst into action, using his sleeve to try and wipe some of the mud away so he could reveal the part that read

NOTICE: THIS IS A NUCLEAR BALL. But some of the mud was harder to remove than other bits, and all he did was now reveal the words:

> ## NOT
> ## A
> ## NUCLEAR BALL

'Act disappointed!' said Hamish, his wild black hair thrashing around in the wind as the airship creaked and groaned in the sky. 'Keep saying "Nuclear Ball"!'

'OH, NO!' yelled Venk, giving it a go. 'THEY'RE GOING TO GET OUR NUCLEAR BALL!'

'YES!' said Alice. 'WHICH THIS DEFINITELY IS!'

She pointed at it for clarity.

'I AGREE!' added Clover, desperately. 'WHAT A PITY THIS **NUCLEAR BALL** IS SO MUDDY AND DIFFICULT TO IDENTIFY AS A NUCLEAR BALL!'

'WORRY NOT!' yelled Elliot. 'ITS NUCLEAR CAPABILITIES WILL NOT BE RADICALLY DIMINISHED!'

But, even while shouting, their voices were tiny and drowned out by the VOOVs from the ship above.

Vinnie sank low into his trolley, staring up at the Superiors' craft, growling like a scared but angry dog and cowering beneath the tartan flap.

'It's not going to work,' said Hamish, his face falling. 'They're not going to go for it!'

'Believe, Hamish,' said Alice. 'We've done all we can. This has to work!'

Then, from nowhere: a shaft of green light shot from the airship and surrounded the fake Nuclear Ball. The light stretched upwards like a tunnel.

The kids stepped back.

What was this? A gamma ray? A laser?

The ball began to shake and quake. Mud flew from it to reveal the paint and metal panels underneath. It looked

like a Nuclear Ball again. Maybe the Superiors
thought the kids had tried to disguise it with mud and dirt!
The ball started to rise, and gently spin, and now it was
halfway between the kids and the airship, suspended in
the air.

'It's working,' said Alice. 'See, Hamish? They're taking it
aboard!'

But Hamish knew something was wrong.

The ball wasn't travelling upwards any more. It was just
hanging there, spinning.

Bright red lasers shot from every corner of the airship and
found the ball, tracing round its edges and moving right the
way across it.

'They're scanning it,' said Elliot. 'They're checking its
properties!'

'It'll be okay,' said Alice, more to herself than anyone. 'It
has to be.'

And then a moment of silence.

Followed by **BWAAAAA-HAAAAAA-HAAAAAAA-HAAAAAAAA!**

The laughter broadcast from the Superiors' tannoys shook
the very ground the kids stood on. Part of the cliff seemed

to creak and crack beneath them.

Were they laughing because they thought they'd found what they came for?

Or because they knew it wasn't?

A moment later, the shaft of green light disappeared and the ball DROPPED to the ground with a **KA-THUD**.

Mud flew everywhere and the kids had their answer.

They'd thought they could outsmart the Superiors. The Superiors had outsmarted them. The Superiors would always outsmart them.

Now a new green shaft of light appeared and surrounded Hamish.

'Hamish!' screamed Alice, trying to pull him out of it.

The Superiors were going to take him instead of the ball. They were going to kidnap the son of Belasko's number-one agent.

He could already feel that his feet were a few centimetres off the ground.

'Grab him!' yelled Buster, and the rest of the **PDF** leapt around Hamish, pulling his shoulders down and clinging onto his feet.

And, though he should have felt terrified, Hamish just felt

small and silly and stupid.

Of course they'd have known that this was just a big sweet. How could Hamish have thought they wouldn't have realised it was just a big sweet and not a giant Nuclear Ball?

Now he had to accept his fate.

He looked at his friends. At poor, hard-working Alice, who'd taught him so much. At Buster, so full of hope. Even at Vinnie, this poor little spytrap who would now doubtless suffer at the hands of his old masters. He'd probably be put straight back in a spytrap field, and be kept starving, and whipped, and made to feel awful all his life and then scoffed with some ketchup. Whatever happened to Hamish and Starkley, poor Vinnie would suffer too. At least Hamish had shown him some kindness. Poor thing must be terrified, thought Hamish, selflessly, as, despite the best efforts of his friends, he continued to slowly rise.

But Vinnie did not look terrified.

He looked defiant.

'SCRAAAAAWWWL!!!'

He began to rise out of his shopping trolley, as Hamish gently spun in the air, seeing his friends, then the water . . . his friends, then the water . . .

And, as he looked into the rough and violent sea, at the sea he knew so well but felt he might be looking at for the very last time, he spotted the crash of unusual waves in the distance.

Something occurred to him.

'Vinnie,' he shouted, snapping out of it, 'scream again!'

'What are you doing?' yelled Alice, still holding onto his shoelaces. 'You're being kidnapped and you're asking a plant to scream?'

Hamish did his best impression of a spytrap scream.

'SCRAAAAAAWWWL!' he yelled, flapping his arms. 'SCRAAAAAWL!'

It was quite clear to his friends that, under all this pressure, Hamish had gone mad.

'Come on!' screamed Hamish to the others, as Alice finally lost her grip. 'SCRAAAAAWL!'

'Scrawl?' said Alice.

'Louder!' urged Hamish, and the gang all joined in, because at this stage, why not?

And then Vinnie understood what they wanted him to do.

'SCRAAAAAAWWWWL!' he shrieked, waving his great viney arms.

'SCRAAAAAWWWWL!'

The piercing scream nearly popped the odd eardrum, but it cut through the **VOOOVS** and was carried along on the wind.

'SCRAWWWL!' yelled Elliot and Buster and Venk.

'SCRAAAAAWL!' yelled Vinnie.

And, a moment later, in the sea, the waves began to rise ...

'SCRAAAWWL!' yelled Hamish, arms flapping. 'Keep going!'

'SCRAAAAAAAAWWWWL!'
shrieked Vinnie, **LOUDER** than ever, and it was at that moment that the **PDF** felt the thunder of powerful waves tumble towards the shore and **SMASH** against the cliffs.

Water and seaweed and whelks and small confused crabs flew through the air.

The sea monster rose from the watery depths.

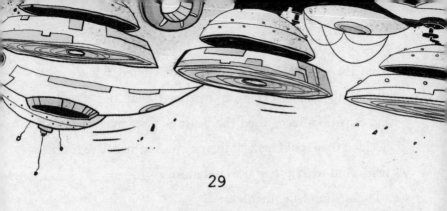

29

FWARP!

The salt water had obviously been very healthy for the Venus spytrap that now towered above them.

It had grown to an unbelievable height and stood rigid, unaffected by the wind and waves that whipped around it.

It dripped with seaweed and moss.

Its thick arms were covered in blistering barnacles and there was an old bicycle wedged between its colossal beige teeth.

The airship had started to turn when it saw it, turning off its shaft of green light in a panic and sending poor Hamish tumbling to the ground. He landed on the **NUCLEAR BALL** and bounced off.

The airship had almost trembled when the plant appeared

from the seabed, but now it regained its confidence and turned to face it. Hamish reckoned that the moment the Superiors recognised the beast as a spytrap, they had decided they could make it their own. Another slave for the field! And what a feast it would make . . .

The spytrap had other ideas.

It crashed its great head down into the water, sending huge waves pounding onto the shore, and flinging the seaweed from its face to get a better look at the airship and whatever had apparently been calling for it.

Down on the cliffs, it blinked as it registered a tiny Venus spytrap called Vinnie, plus a smattering of those strange miniature human things.

It roared.

'SCRAAAAAAAWWWWLLL!'

Hundreds of fish flew from its mouth, followed by muck and old plastic bags and another bicycle.

'Hamish,' whispered Alice. 'I'm not sure this was one of your better ideas.'

'Somehow,' added Elliot, 'you have made a bad situation even worse.'

The PDF were spattered by gunk as the monster drew closer . . . *BOOM BOOM BOOM* . . . pulling its

246

own roots through the muddy ocean floor, carving it up like a tractor carves up a field.

The airship flew lower now, with Terribles pressed up against the windows, and Superiors barking instructions. They were excited. They hadn't expected to grow their own sea monster. The complete destruction of Earth was going to be so much easier now!

'Hold still,' said Hamish. 'Show it no fear!'

But even Vinnie was cowering now. He shuddered as the giant version of himself lowered one ginormous head until it was just centimetres from his own, and one more time . . .

'SCRAAAAAAWWWWWWLLLLLL!'

The kids' hair all blew back from the force of its call.

Its breath was hideous. Its eyes were black. The sea had done nothing to blunt its sharp teeth.

'Now, Vinnie,' whispered Hamish. 'Now!'

Shaking, Vinnie found his confidence.

He stretched himself taller.

And said . . .

'mew.'

The giant spytrap blinked, twice.

Vinnie tried again.

'mew mew.'

'**BUUUUHF?**' roared the beast.

'mewmewmew!' said Vinnie, his bravery growing.

The giant spytrap began to snortle and sniff. Great puffs of black smoke covered the kids in soot.

Alice stared. Were Vinnie and the giant spytrap . . . communicating?

'**BEAST!**' came the voice of the Superiors over the tannoy. '**BE STILL! DESTROY THE HUMANS! JOIN YOUR MASTERS!**'

'mew mew' said Vinnie, nodding up at the airship, at those who had been so cruel to their kind. He threw his leafy arms back and forth as he did so.

'Vinnie,' whispered Hamish and then he nodded towards the Nuclear Ball.

Vinnie continued his chatter and, as he did so, the giant trap snapped its head upwards, to stare at the airship above.

It took in the Superiors, studied the nasty, awful Terribles pressed up against each window, almost slathering in anticipation, their greasy, fat fingers tightening round their whips.

'**BOW DOWN!**' screamed the Superiors. '**BOW DOWN TO US!**'

The spytrap took one more look at Vinnie.

Vinnie stared up at it.

Then the spytrap **LUUURCHED** towards the children, its mouth open, its huge fangs dripping and gleaming.

'It's going to **EAT US!**' screamed Venk.

And, just as Hamish was about to say his final goodbyes, the beast **CHAMPED** its teeth round the Nuclear Ball, whipped its head back and flung it straight at the airship!

Through the air it flew!

A direct hit!

The airship rocked and groaned as the speeding ball ripped through its side.

Two of its motors stopped, and it tipped from left to right, as the Superiors struggled to control it.

'It just needs to hit the water tank!' said Hamish. 'If it can just hit the—'

BOOOOOOOOOOOOM!

The biggest boom you've ever heard! In fact, it was more like:

Thundering great splinters of wood and plastic and metal spun and twirled through the air. The oversized Scandi Candgrenade had worked! The airship turned and tried to fly, but it was no good . . . this airship was an airship no longer.

BOOOM! CCCHH! POW! it went, as the deadly, industrial-strength Norwegian popping candy did its business. Colourful shards of ship and candy streaked through the air, twizzling about, exploding over the sea.

This was the greatest fireworks display Starkley had ever seen!

'It worked!' screamed Alice, punching the air. 'Hamish! It worked!'

Dozens of tiny emergency escape pods shot from the side of the airship, as it thundered down towards the waves. The pods weren't hanging around – they were obviously programmed to head straight back to Venus the second they were released.

More and more of them left the craft and shot through the sky, up into the cosmos, flashing as they left the atmosphere, leaving only chaos behind them.

The empty airship crashed into the sea, sending heavy waves rocketing upwards.

The monster, Vinnie and the kids all stared up into the sky.

They had done it.

They should be very proud of themselves.

And they were.

Until they realised that just because the Superiors had gone, that didn't mean they were entirely . . . well . . . safe.

Sure, they'd worked with a monster to rid the world of danger.

But that still left them standing totally alone on a cliff top . . . with a monster.

Slowly, the gargantuan aquatic spytrap lowered its mammoth head to take in the small group once more.

It stared at the children. Licked its enormous lips.

Hamish and the **PDF** began to back away, hiding behind Vinnie.

'**MEW?**' said the beast, nodding at the children, and now looking rather hungrier than it had before.

'**MEW.**' said Vinnie, sternly, making himself bigger, spreading his little leafy arms, shaking his head.

A moment passed.

Then the giant beast nodded slightly, turned and stalked off, back into the sea, the hunt for fish and moss and rusty old bikes very much back on.

As it disappeared under the waves, nearby the airship groaned as it sank, massive pockets and bubbles of air rising to the surface of the sea with an extremely surprising

FWWWWWWAAAAAAAARRRRRPPPP.

And the **PDF** began to shake with the glorious pure laughter of relief, as Elliot said, 'Told you there'd be a GravityFart!'

30

Return to Starkley

Halfway through the **PDF**'s triumphant walk home, Hamish's dad was speeding down the road in his Belasko lorry until all sixteen wheels skidded to a halt. Great plumes of smoke rose from behind it as the tyre rubber marked the road.

'Hamish!' yelled Dad, jumping out. 'Kids!'

'Dad!' said Hamish. 'Did you see?'

'Did I see?' he said. 'Did I see you take on the Superiors?'

Hamish nodded, delighted.

'Did I see you raise a sea monster?' said Dad. 'Yes, I saw, Hamish. And I was amazed!'

But Hamish's dad didn't look like he was happy to be amazed.

'I was amazed because I told you not to do anything. I told you to wait!'

The **PDF** all looked at each other. Were they in trouble? How could they be in trouble after all that?

'Do you have any idea how dangerous that was?' said Hamish's dad. 'It's one thing coming up with a plan, son. And I even let you be part of it. But it's another thing entirely to do what you did. Particularly when I said not to!'

Hamish had been staring at the ground as his dad spoke.

But then he looked up, like some fire had been lit inside him.

'Do you know what, Dad?' said Hamish, sternly, which was not like him at all. 'I'm angry with you too.'

Angus Ellerby stopped in his tracks. These weren't words he'd ever heard from his son before. He knew that deep inside Hamish there must have been some anger from when he'd had to disappear.

And maybe it was finally coming out.

'I'm really angry, because you don't seem to trust me as much as you should,' said Hamish, almost trembling. 'You should be proud, not angry.'

Alice put a hand on Hamish's back. Not to stop him, but to help him find the strength.

'Look at me,' said Hamish. 'Look at the **PDF**. Think about everything we've done in the past.'

His dad kneeled down, so that they were at eye level.

'I get that sometimes you have to leave me behind,' said Hamish. 'But I'm scared you'll go away again, or that something will happen to you. When you went away that first time, I know it's just because you love me. And when you wanted us to stay in town and do nothing, I understand that it's just because you love me. When you said you wanted us all to leave Starkley, I understand that it's just because you love me.'

His dad nodded, softly.

'But I love you,' said Hamish. 'And I love Mum. And I even love Jimmy most of the time, even though I do not think he has a future in spoken-word poetry. And I love my friends and I love Starkley. And they're things worth fighting for, not hiding from.'

The wind whipped around Hamish's hair as his dad stared

into his eyes and thought about what to say next.

And then he smiled.

'You're right,' he said. 'I don't ever want you to think you can't tell me things. You should always say how you feel. Never hide it. And what you did was incredible. What you all did.'

Hamish smiled at his friends. They were a great team, and now they'd proved it more than ever.

'I mean, as your dad, I have to say it could have gone so wrong,' he added, before catching himself. 'But, as a **Belasko** agent, I have to say I'm so proud of you. There was the Before. Then there was the Now. But the Then? That was up for grabs. This could have been the Superiors' world, or ours, Hamish. You and your pals made sure it was ours.'

Normally, he'd have ruffled Hamish's hair at this point. But now he stood tall, and held out his hand for Hamish to shake.

'You were right to tell me not to give up on Starkely. And you were absolutely right to do what you did. And I have always been proud of you.'

And just then, Hamish felt pretty important.

I wish I could tell you that they got home to a huge party, with balloons and party poppers and those disgusting iced biscuits that you seem to like so much, but the truth was Starkley was in quite a mess.

Only now that things were getting back to normal did Hamish realise just what an effect the GravityBurps had had.

There was rubbish all over the place. Windows that had cracked under pressure. Tree branches that had broken off and now lay forgotten in the street. And brick dust all over the place from when the buildings had transformed.

But, when the **PDF** climbed out of Dad's lorry, Hamish immediately forgot about all that. The whole town came out to cheer their heroes.

Mr Longblather. Dr Fussbundler. Madame Cous Cous. The whole of Winterbourne School. Kids, parents and even old Mr Neate stood around them and applauded.

'My brave, incredible boy!' said his mum, rushing out of the council offices, picking Hamish up and spinning him round. 'What kids you are!'

'It wasn't just us,' said Hamish, blushing. 'There was Vinnie. And a certain sea monster. And we mustn't forget the other heroes of the hour: the Norwegians!'

Erik and Viktor Viktorius stepped forward and each did a little bow.

'It's just nice to feel useful!' said Erik. 'Not even Norwegian kids want Norwegian candies any more.'

He made a sad face. Way to kill a mood, Erik.

'Well,' said Dad. 'I guess we set to work cleaning up the town!'

Everyone cheered, even though that sounded rubbish.

And then the put-put-put of a small engine coming around the corner filled the air.

'Oh, no!' said Mum, guessing what it would be. 'Not now!'

A small van turned the corner and came into view.

On its side was written **PUBLIC OFFICE OF PRIDE**.

And in the driver's seat was a burly woman with a teetering pink beehive.

'It's Goonhilda Swag!' yelled Mum. 'Come to close the town!'

'SURPRISE!' shouted Goonhilda, struggling to get her seat belt over her neck cone, and stumbling out of the van. 'This is the SURPRISE VISIT I warned you about!'

Everyone took a step back as she walked towards them, a sneery grin taking over her face.

'Oh, dear,' she said, thrilled. 'Oh, dear, oh, dear, oh, dear.'

She whipped out a clipboard from somewhere behind her and began to make notes.

'Brick dust. Inadequate refuse control. Broken windows.' She tittered. 'An upside-down car. Bits of old tree contravening health-and-safety regulations. A strange, grotesque old man.'

Mr Neate frowned.

'Everyone outside all at once, causing a fire hazard.'

'We were just about to clean up,' said Hamish's mum. 'You see, Ms Swag, we've had quite a couple of days . . .'

'What has happened to the sweet shop?' said Goonhilda. 'Why is it now a science laboratory? Did you get planning permission for that? And what on earth has happened to the town clock? Someone appears to have turned it into an intercontinental ballistic missile!'

She looked shocked now, rather than happy. She had never had a case like this before. It was like Starkley had wilfully changed itself into something that went against everything the **Public Office of Pride** stood for. This was a direct challenge to her authority. These people were mocking her! They had no respect! No respect at all! Well, she would teach them a lesson all right. She would shut this town down!

'Right!' she said, walking over to where Hamish and the **PDF** were standing. 'You can witness this. I am about to sign a document which will go straight to the Queen and inform her that your town is to be struck off the map!'

She was talking so loudly and with such force that she didn't hear the sniffing noise from behind her.

'You will **RUE THE DAY** you messed with Goonhilda Swag!' she yelled, and so mesmerised was she by her own words she didn't notice the shadow creeping over her shoulder from the small tartan trolley she'd paid no attention to. Nor did she feel the wet tang of saliva in the air . . .

'Vinnie!' said Hamish. 'No!'

But Vinnie was hungry. And as he slowly rose from his tartan shopping trolley he did not see a human being. He saw a neck cone with a pink beehive on top. A sight which to his little beady eyes looked exactly the same as a cone of candyfloss!

CHOMP!

For a second, no one said anything.

And then Goonhilda Swag blinked, twice.

She dropped her clipboard and raised her little fat hands to her head.

'My beehive!' she yelled. 'What's happened to my beehive?'

She turned to see a giant, toothy, man-eating plant munching quite happily on what appeared to be a small pink poodle.

She felt her head. Her barnet had gone! He'd made her look like Friar Tuck!

'I HATE THIS TOWN!' she screamed.

And then Goonhilda Swag fainted.

When she woke up, poor Goonhilda decided it must all have been a terrible dream.

For, when she came to, on a bench in the middle of town, she saw a Starkley that was so beautiful she couldn't understand how she could ever have had anything against it.

It was the picture-perfect British village.

Thatched cottages everywhere. A gentle sun glistening on a river she'd never noticed before. Around her, elderly couples danced around a maypole, waving handkerchiefs and jangling bells. Two little boys were scrumping for apples in a happy vicar's back garden. A local bobby tipped his helmet at her.

'Starkley is . . . charming!' she said. 'Quite charming!'

'I'm so pleased you like it,' said Hamish's mum, standing beside her. 'It's our home and, well, we love it.'

'Oh, I can see why!' said Goonhilda, who caught sight of herself in the window of Madame Cous Cous's International World of Treats and admired her own tall tower of pink hair. What had she been thinking before? Perhaps it had been that fish sandwich she bought from the motorway cafe on the way here. It had clearly affected her thinking! 'Well, rest assured that I will tell the Queen what a wonderful place this is! I will tell her at once!'

'Thank you,' said Hamish's dad, opening the door of Goonhilda's van and helping her in. 'Have a safe journey home.'

Goonhilda Swag started her engine, and happily put-put-putted away and out of Starkley forever.

'Okay,' said Alice. 'I'd better turn off the Holonow.'

VVSSSHEEEW.

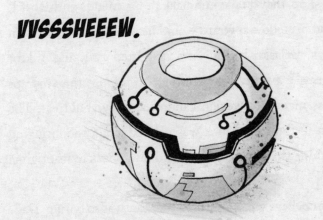

Starkley returned to normal.

'And so begins the clear-up,' said Hamish's mum, with a happy sigh.

'How long before she notices her hair, Mum?' asked Hamish.

They'd had to wait for Vinnie to cough up Goonhilda's beehive like a wet hairball. Madame Cous Cous dried it with six hairdryers, and then attached it to Goonhilda's head with sixty pieces of Billericay Bubble Gum – chewed until sticky by all the children in Hamish's year.

'Let's just hope that's the last we've seen of her,' said Mum, looking relaxed for the first time in ages.

Belasko agents were helping clean up Starkley, and had more news too. Once Vinnie had had his fill of the sweet shop, they'd take him back to his friends on FRYKT. He and his fellow spytraps would be well looked after from now on. Belasko had given a delighted Erik and Viktor Viktorius a twenty-year contract to supply the spytraps with as many Norwegian candies as they could eat. The button in the town clock was pressed again too, bringing everything that Hamish knew and loved back to its original state.

'I can't believe you let us think Starkley was so boring, Dad,' said Hamish, as his dad joined the agents and townsfolk in clearing up.

'We felt pretty guilty about it,' said Dad. 'That's why we

always made sure you at least had a sweet shop, and the fair visited once a year.'

He ruffled Hamish's hair.

'In fact,' he said, looking at his watch, 'I made a call to Belasko Fun Incorporated, and . . .'

From nowhere, a dozen lorries noisily rolled into town and, once the kids saw what they were, they couldn't stop cheering.

On the side of each lorry was the fairground ride they were carrying.

GRANDMA'S REVENGE.

And Hamish's favourite:

The GAP-TOOTHED OTTER.

The fair was back in town. Just for them. Just for today.

'Off you go,' said Dad, smiling, as Buster, Alice, Clover, Elliot and Venk chased after the lorries, punching the air.

'Are you sure you don't want help tidying up?' asked Hamish.

'Hamish,' said Dad. 'You saved the world. Three times. It's time you just enjoyed being a kid again.'

Of course, somewhere out there, on Venus or perhaps Neptune, the Superiors would be licking their wounds and making new plans, probably joined by Axel Scarmarsh and a band of ghastly Terribles. A new threat may rise. They always do.

But that would be a problem for another day.

As his mum cuddled into his dad, Hamish Ellerby ran off to join his friends, with a very special new mission indeed: to just enjoy being a kid again.

DJ JIMMY LYRICIS

FEATURING THE HIT SONGS:

IS IT SAUSAGES FOR
TEA AGAIN?

THE BALLAD OF
FELICITY GOBB?

I HAVE A QUESTION - WHY DO
I SAY EVERYTHING LIKE IT'S
A QUESTION (ALTHOUGH THAT
IS AN ACTUAL QUESTION)?

RHyME TIME

PARENTAL
ADVISORY
EXPLICIT CONTENT

VISIT FRYKT!

Come and feed the
spytraps some quality
Norwegian sweets!
It is literally the only way
we'll get rid of them.

THE FAIR IS BACK IN STARKLEY

WHO DARES TAKE ON...

GRANDMA'S REVENGE???

R. DIDDUMS
For the fashion-conscious baby

ALL STOCK COMPLETELY SOLD OUT

* * * Baby berets * * *
* * * Baby monocles * * *
* * Baby sweetcorn * *

STARKLEY
♥ ♥ LOVE ♥ ♥
CONNECTIONS

Are you the tiny red
man I met in the school
hall? We seemed to get
on like a house on fire.
Maybe we could meet
and ignite the flames of
love? – Madame C.C.

p14. New book about anti-gravity! Impossible to put down.

P3b. Who is Andromeda Star? And is it true there's a space hotel?

P07. Record births in Starkley! It's a baby blizzard!

NOW APPROVED BY THE PUBLIC OFFICE OF PRIDE (POOP)

Starkley Post

Wednesday 28st issue 12 vol XX

Price: 92p

WHAT WAS THAT?

Complaints have been flooding in to Starkley Town Council about crazy lights coming from Garage 5 of Slackjaw's Motors.

'Is he having a disco in there?' asked local resident Brittle Gubbins. 'Lights of all colours flicker on for a minute or so and then lots of smoke appears around the edges.'

Pensioner Gum Spittle has seen it too.

'If he's having discos in there, he should be honest about it, because I love dancing but the police told me I wasn't allowed to any more because my moves are too wonderful and some are so powerful they can make people's legs go all soupy.'

So far Mr Slackjaw has denied any knowledge of any late-night discos taking place in Garage 5 and said he doesn't even like garage music.

But neighbours remain sure something's going on…

BRITISH HAIRWAYS

Cone and get the hairstyle everyone's talking about!

THE GOONHILDA!

Now with free neck cone!

Hamish Ellerby Would Like to Thank…

… the following brave Belasko souls for their tireless and often unseen devotion in furthering the cause of the Pause Defense Force. General Jane Griffiths; Brigadiers Elisa Offord and Laura Hough; Colonel Jack Noel; Majors Robert Kirby and Ariella Feiner; and the Officer Cadets of Simon & Schuster, London, and all who sail in them. Hamish should also like to thank Lieutenant Elliot Wallace in particular, whose walk around a garden centre on Englefield Road one brisk weekend led to the immediate invention of a certain alien plant…

HAMISH
ELLERBY

WILL RETURN...

www.worldofhamish.com